COSCOM
ENTERTAINMENT

BIGFOOT

VOLUME TWO

TERROR TALES

EDITED BY

ERIC S. BROWN AND A.P. FUCHS

COSCOM ENTERTAINMENT

WINNIPEG

The fiction in this book is just that: fiction. Names, characters, places and events either are products of the author's imagination or are used fictitiously. Any resemblance to actual events or persons living or dead, or any known Sasquatches is purely coincidental.

ISBN 978-1-927339-07-7

Published by COSCOM ENTERTAINMENT
www.coscomentertainment.com
Text set in Garamond; Printed and Bound in the USA

COVER ART BY GARY MCCLUSKEY
EDITING CONSULTANT: KEITH GOUVEIA

Table of Contents

SEPARATION ANXIETY

BY

KEITH GOUVEIA

WITH ONE HAND over his mouth and the other pulling his mate along with him, he ran through the grayish haze. Their thunderous footsteps helping to snuff out tiny embers that sparked off the trees. The only thing visible in the dense smoke was the orange glow of the roaring fire. Surrounded by its crackle, he was lost. They had gotten turned around and twisted too many times—due to the fire's quickness—that keeping track of their location proved daunting.

When the first hint of sulfur hit their nostrils, they ran into action to do what they could to put out the fire and save their home. On the way, deer, bears, birds, raccoons and squirrels passed them, all fleeing for their lives.

The fire ravaging the forest was unlike any he had ever seen before. The rains had been sparse over the course of the year, and most of the undergrowth had become quick kindling. The acrid stink of burning sandalwood, cedar, and moss mixed with his own musk set his lungs and throat ablaze; his eyes watered, blurring his field of vision.

Must go!

His muscles ached to the point of breaking as his heart thundered in his chest. But he needed to be strong. To endure. The sobs of his love instilled a sense of urgency within him. He had to get her out safely and back to their children. It was his job—his *responsibility*. He pressed on, hoping he was heading in the right direction and praying their children were outside of the fire's reach.

The creaking of a falling tree drowned out the roar of the fire, its leaves rustling as it passed through the forest's canopy. He stopped and listened, his head pivoting left and right as he tried to decipher the tree's trajectory.

In his peripheral vision he caught sight of it, and in the split second he had before the tree crushed him and his love, he pulled her by the arm and tossed her to safety with disregard to his own. The fiery oak struck his shoulder, igniting his senses in pain. He crashed to the forest floor, pinned under its weight.

With his palms against the bark he pushed the glowing red bark, but the exertion caused shockwaves of pain to ripple throughout his body, originating from his chest. Instead, he patted out the nearby embers to avoid being burned.

His love cried out for him as she rushed to his side. She leaped over the large tree trunk effortlessly, knelt down beside him, and cradled his head in her hands. Her tears splashed upon his cheek and ran across his lips. In their salty tang, he could almost taste her love for him. He tried to speak, but the weight across his chest made breathing difficult.

The sound of more trees creaking off in the distance reminded him of the danger. He lifted his head out of her embrace and took her hand in his, then pushed it aside. She looked at him with a wrinkled brow and confusion in her eyes. He grunted and pointed in the other direction.

She shook her head and clutched his hand in hers.

With his free hand, he brushed a trickling tear off her cheek. He looked deep into her brown eyes and thought of their children. How he was going to miss seeing them grow up, and how he wouldn't be there to teach them to hunt and fend for themselves.

As if seeing his thoughts in his eyes, his love released her hold on his hand and stood. He grunted again and shooed her away. She slouched forward and gripped the tree. From his position, he could see the strain on her face, but he knew she was not as strong as him. After a few seconds, she punched the tree and sent another shockwave of pain throughout his body. He moaned and she gasped as she realized what she had done. She stepped toward him and he shook his head. Tears pooled in her eyes as she reached out with a shaky hand. He waved his hand in return, signaling for her to run.

With a heavy sob, she turned away and ran. He watched her for as long as he could before the grayish haze consumed her.

As he lay there, blanketed by smoke, he thought of happier times: bouncing his baby boy and girl on his knees; carrying them on his shoulders and running as fast as he could, letting the wind kiss their cheeks and blow through their auburn hair; the laughing and splashing during bath time. A fit of reflexive coughing distracted him from the memory.

His breaths were becoming shorter and his throat was hoarse. Numbness crept over his mind as a wave of nausea roiled in his stomach. The weight on his chest grew heavier as his body struggled for oxygen. He looked up at the forest's canopy; the trees seemed to swirl together.

The smoke burned his eyes. He blinked them in rapid succession, but it did no good.

Sleep.

He needed sleep to regain his strength. He closed his eyes to the world, the image of his beloved prominent in his mind's eye.

◆　◆　◆

In all his years as a firefighter with the Adams County Fire Department, Matthew Roland had never seen such devastation. The forest floor, black with soot and ash, was muddy from the aerial water drops. It clung to his yellow boots, adding extra weight. The few stragglers of plant life remaining were brown and withered; the only green visible was up in the treetops, far beyond the fire's reach.

It'll be a long while before things are remotely close to what they were, he thought. *And to think, three punks caused all of this.* He shook his head at the senselessness of it all.

The fire was started in Minnesota and spread outward from there. It threatened the Canadian border and branched into Wisconsin. Every firefighter in three states was called to the scene and a massive front was established. They attacked the fire by air and ground as a cohesive unit.

Off in the distance, through the clear-face mask, he saw a bulldozer tilling the forest floor, snuffing out any remaining embers, the smoky haze nowhere near as dense as it had been during the fire's peak. Matthew took a deep breath of clean oxygen and scouted for the other unit; in case of an emergency he wanted to know their position. He spotted them off to the right, heading further east.

Hope they don't go too far, he thought, then focused on his current path.

At his side were veteran firefighter Nick Charles and rookie Murphy Prager. Armed with their axes and adorned in their heavy protective gear, Matthew's legs were starting to feel the strain and he wondered how the new kid was holding up. Out in the wild, the normal, hardened leather helmet was traded in for a tougher, ballistic nylon one capable of protecting them from falling trees or heavy branches.

"Where's your head at, Matt?" asked Nick, obviously sensing his distraction.

"I'm just disgusted. Going to be a long while before I can take Jimmy out here."

"Yeah. I know what you mean," said Murphy. "My father used to take me hunting out here all the time in the summers."

"It's what all the men do," added Nick.

How true, Matthew thought. He couldn't count the number of camping trips he had taken his son on in the forest surrounding the Great Lakes. The fishing and the hunting—two men living off the land the way God intended—so many wonderful memories that helped forge an everlasting bond.

"I see a soft glow over there." Murphy pointed toward the left.

Matthew and Nick both turned to see for themselves.

"We better head over there," said Nick, taking the first step.

"Should we call the others?" asked Murphy.

"Let's wait and see. It looks small enough from here."

When they reached the small grouping of bushes still ablaze, Matthew and Murphy immediately started tossing dirt onto the flames while Nick wandered a few yards up ahead.

Typical, Matthew thought, then tapped Murphy on the shoulder and signaled him to step back. With one swing of his axe, the first bush toppled over, and in three more swings, the group was separated and more easily managed.

"Guys! Check this out!"

"You think he found another fire?" Murphy asked.

Matthew shrugged his shoulders and stomped on the bush one last time with his size-thirteen boot before walking over toward Nick.

"He probably found a perfectly protected crop of marijuana," said Murphy.

"No doubt, right?" Matthew said, and then felt his bottom jaw dangle open.

"Is that a man?"

Murphy's question went unanswered as Matthew stared at a pair of the longest, hairiest legs he had ever seen jutting out from underneath a massive oak tree. The legs were attached to feet the size of his forearm and pointing toward the heavens.

Nick was on the other side of the fallen tree, and as he climbed over the trunk, he saw a creature of myth and legend. There was no mistaking what lay dead underneath the oak.

Could it be? Matthew thought as his gaze fixated on the ridge just above the creature's brow, with its large, low-set forehead. Covered in reddish hair, a single crest bone ran lengthwise along the midline of its huge head. The lips and chin blended together and hung past the upper jaw, and Matthew couldn't help but think it had been dislocated upon impact with the tree. *There's just no other explanation . . . but how?*

"Looks like some kind of ape," said Murphy.

"It's friggin' Bigfoot! Hot damn!" Nick said, slapping his hands together, then jumping up and kicking his heels. "We're gonna be rich, boys!"

Matthew just looked upon his partner in disbelief. Here he was, trembling inside, while the old man shouted out with childish glee.

"You think it's dead?" Murphy asked.

Nick put his hands on his hips. "How should I know? Check it for a pulse."

Murphy stepped back. "I ain't touching it."

Nick looked to Matthew.

"Hey, you're the one with dreams of grandeur."

Nick flared his nostrils as he sucked in his gut and fiddled with his belt—the stance he always took before pulling rank. "Rookie, it's an order."

Murphy's throat muscles flexed as if he was swallowing his fear. His eyes wide, he stared at the unconscious behemoth. He curled his hands into fists as he nibbled on his lower lip.

"Get on with it!"

"Easy, Nick, can't you see he's scared?"

Nick shook his head. "Pansy."

With a deep breath, Murphy kicked one of the massive feet.

Silence befell the men as all eyes were upon the creature, searching for any sign of life.

None came.

"Live or dead, it's still worth a butt-load," Nick said, breaking the eerie silence.

"Are we just going to bring someone here or—" Matthew started.

"You crazy?" Nick said. "They'll want a cut. No. We need to bring it in ourselves."

"And how do we do that?" asked Murphy. "That tree's gotta weigh a ton."

"Yeah." Nick scratched his chin.

"We'll get the chainsaw from the truck. Cut the tree into smaller, more manageable pieces."

"Good idea, Matthew . . . but who's gonna go?" Murphy asked, looking to each one of them.

"I'll go," said Nick. "I don't trust either of you to not squeal like little girls gossiping in the schoolyard."

"Hey!" Murphy said, stretching the word.

"Nothing personal, kid."

"Whatever."

Matthew simply laughed at the two of them. It had been this way for the past three months. Nick belittled the younger Murphy, hazed him at the station with childish antics such as gluing his pen caps shut, relocating his locker in the line-up, and changing the language setting of his cell-phone. But Murphy took it in stride and only taunted Nick with questions of retirement and the need for a certain blue pill in order to satisfy his old lady. Despite this, Matthew knew there was mutual respect.

"So what do we do?" asked Murphy as Nick started his trek back toward Route 2 where the trucks were stationed.

"I don't know. I suppose we do what we're supposed to and look for any kindling underbrush."

"What about him?" Murphy asked, pointing toward the creature.

"He ain't going anywhere. But we'll stay close."

Murphy nodded in understanding, then turned to circle the perimeter.

As Matthew made a move to walk away, he thought he saw the creature's hand twitch in his peripheral vision. He stopped and stared at the rock-sized fist.

When no movement came, he released the breath he had been holding. *Just my anxiety playing tricks on me*, he thought. *There's no way it could have survived the night. It surely would have died from smoke inhalation.*

The creature's fingers uncurled and Matthew jumped back, frightened by the sudden movement.

Get a hold of yourself.

Matthew released his fear and allowed his training and experience to kick in. He quickly removed his facemask as he stepped toward the creature. With his mask off, he knelt down beside it and placed the mask over its mouth and nose. Precious oxygen seeped from the sides as the ridge of the mask barely reached the creature's brow. He knew the creature wasn't getting the full effect, but he hoped it was enough.

Slowly, the creature pumped its fingers as it regained consciousness. Its eyes fluttered open and upon seeing him, its giant body jolted with shock. It knocked the facemask away and pushed against the trunk of the tree.

"*Easy*, big guy," he said in the softest voice he could muster. He placed a gentle hand on the creature's muscular shoulder. Its auburn fur was rough like the bristles of a brush. "I'm not going to hurt you."

It looked deep into his eyes and with a look of realization, Matthew felt its muscles relax under his touch.

"Would you like some water?" he asked as he fumbled for the canteen strapped to his waist. With the round container in hand, he twisted the top off, then placed one hand behind the creature's head while he brought the canteen to its lips. With a tip, water cascaded out of the canteen's mouth and past the large, plump lips of the Bigfoot.

Its hands shot toward the canteen and tipped it further. The Bigfoot greedily drank, and Matthew let him have his fill.

"Okay," he said, pulling the canteen from its lips. "Let's save some for later."

The creature swallowed hard, then wiped its mouth with the back of its hand.

"You're going to need this, though." Matthew reached over the creature's broad chest and snatched his facemask, then returned it to the Bigfoot's face. The creature placed his hand over Matthew's, completely swallowing it. "Just a gentle giant, aren't you?"

With his legs beginning to cramp, Matthew sat down; the ground was still warm from the night's fire. As he sat there, feeding clean oxygen to the creature, his gaze fixated on the tree trunk across its chest. There was blood on the bark and its fur was matted along the contact points.

"My friend will be back soon, then we'll get this off you," he said. "You're lucky to be alive."

The creature nodded its head as if understanding.

"Can you . . . nah." *Wish I had an aspirin for him*, he thought. "Hold on," he mumbled as he reached for the radio transmitter clipped to his shoulder. "Nick, you there? Over."

"Yeah. What is it? I'm busy . . . over."

"You're not going to believe this, but . . . grab the first aid kit, too. Over."

"What did the rookie trip on? Over."

"It's not for Murphy." He paused, trying to decide what to say next, not knowing who might be in earshot of Nick.

"You pullin' my leg," came Nick's voice. "Please tell me you're not pullin' my leg. Over."

"No, sir. Over."

"Hot damn! He's worth ten times as much alive."

All the possibilities of what would happen to this majestic beast crossed Matthew's mind. Scientific experiments with possible dissection, or caged and put on display. The notion of this being a bad idea suddenly weighed heavily on his shoulders.

"Listen, Nick, maybe we shouldn't be doing this. Over."

"You friggin' kiddin' me? Think of the money. The fame. Think of your boy not wanting for anything. You better think long and hard about this before I get back. Get your head straight, man. Over and out!"

"Lousy sonuva . . ." Matthew let his thoughts trail off, not wanting the creature to sense his animosity.

Time felt as though it was standing still as he waited for Nick to return with the medical supplies. The Bigfoot proved more patient than Matthew as it lay there quietly and staring upward at the forest canopy. The fur on its broad chest was becoming even more matted as the blood continued to flow and though Matthew was no doctor, he just knew the weight of the large tree was no good for the creature's internal organs. There was just no telling what kinds of injuries were laying under the surface.

Will they treat him before dissecting him? he wondered.

As expected, Murphy was the first to return. "You never left its side, did you?"

"No. Sorry."

"I don't think it matters. Everything's pretty much under control now."

"Well that's good," Matthew said.

"How's he doing?"

Matthew shook his head. "I have no idea."

Murphy walked around the fallen tree and sat beside him. Silence befell them as neither knew what to say and the sound of Nick's grating voice was like music to their ears. His annoying cat call to let them know he was back echoed off the trees. He returned carrying a white metal box in one hand and a chainsaw in the other. Matthew stood and walked toward him to greet him. Murphy followed.

"Everything okay here?" Nick asked as he approached.

"Yeah, give me that," Matthew replied, reaching for the first aid kit.

Nick jerked the case away from Matthew's reach. "Not so fast."

"What's going on?" asked Murphy. His question went ignored.

"Just give it to me."

Nick stopped and placed the chainsaw on the ground, then reached around toward his back. For a split second, Matthew thought he was reaching for a gun. He wouldn't put it past the old man to cut him and Murphy out of the equation and claim the creature for his own.

"We need to restrain it somehow," Nick said, revealing a pair of handcuffs.

"Where'd you get those?" Murphy asked, eyeing the metallic bracelets.

"From the glove compartment of an unmanned squad car parked on the road."

"Should have taken the shotgun, too," Murphy said.

"Couldn't . . . it was locked in place." Nick held out the cuffs and first aid kit.

Without a word, Matthew took the cuffs and the proffered white box from Nick. He returned to Bigfoot's side, dropped to his knees, and popped the latches on the lid. His first priority was making the creature comfortable. Inside, he found the necessary gauze and anti-bacterial ointment in order to treat the creature's chest wound. "What happened to the aspirin?" he asked as he continued to rummage through the first aid kit.

"They took those out for safety reasons. Higher ups didn't want to be responsible for people mixing medications," Nick answered.

"Crap. He needs something for the pain," Matthew said, stroking the wiry hair atop the Bigfoot's head.

"It's just an animal, man. It'll be fine."

Even Murphy had a look of surprise and shock upon his face from Nick's insensitive words.

"How can you be so cruel?" asked the rookie.

"Whatever," Nick said, then mumbled, "bleeding heart liberals."

Matthew just shook his head, then returned his attention to the creature. He eyed the handcuffs at his side. *Guess I have no choice.* "Don't worry," he said as he grabbed the Bigfoot's hand. His own hand looked as though it was a baby's in comparison. He opened the cuffs as wide as they could and tried setting them in place, but no matter where he positioned them along the creature's wrists, they would not close. He tossed them to the ground. "These won't work."

"Why not?" asked Nick.

"He's too big. The clasp won't connect."

Nick threw his hands up. "Fine! Then how are we going to do this?"

"It would probably be best to attack the tree from this side," said Murphy, pointing toward the side facing the uprooted base. "I should be able to slip a log between the ground and the trunk over here, then when the tree is cut in half, we should be able to lift the lighter end up enough to slide the Bigfoot out from underneath it."

Nick's bottom jaw dangled open as he stared at Murphy with wide eyes. "That's gotta be the smartest thing you've ever said, Rookie."

"Thanks," Murphy replied, looking as though he didn't mind the backhanded comment.

"Never mind standing around looking all smug-like—find a log!"

"Yes, sir!"

While Murphy scoured the forest floor for a suitable branch, Nick inspected the chainsaw's blade and spark plug. "Since you two are so close, you'll have to hold it down."

"What?" Matthew asked, fear creeping over him. There was no telling how the vibrations of the chainsaw and the tree trunk would affect the beast and he had no idea what the creature would do to him while it was in excruciating pain.

"You heard me," Nick said, eyes narrowed.

"What's your—?"

"Found one!"

"All right, kid," Nick said as he primed the chainsaw. "Get it in place. You ready, Matt?"

"As I'll ever be, I suppose." He placed a comforting hand on its muscular shoulder. "It'll be all right," he said softly.

When Nick pulled the start cord on the chainsaw and its engine roared to life, the Bigfoot's demeanor changed instantly. Eyes wide and lips pursed, it slapped Matthew's hand away and clawed at the tree trunk atop its chest, desperately trying to wriggle itself free. Deep claw marks ran through the tree bark as a cloud of sawdust filled the air. It tried and tried to push the weight off, but it was useless. Whimpers of terror turned into pleading grunts as the chainsaw's blade continued through the tree trunk and pieces of wood shot out in all directions.

Matthew could only imagine the pain surging in the creature's chest, the vibrations traveling straight through the Bigfoot's frame and possibly expanding the wound hidden from his sight.

"Hurry up, Nick. You're hurting it."

"Dammit, Matt, I can only go so fast."

"Just do what you can."

Matthew's attention returned to the Bigfoot in time to see the beast reaching above its head. His gaze followed the creature's long arm toward the rock it was trying to get. Just as he realized what its intentions were, its fingers curled around the rock and lifted it off the ground.

"Look out!" he shouted.

The rock hurled straight toward Nick's head. Nick, looking as if he hadn't a clue, ducked out of instinct. The rock soared passed him, missing the side of his head by inches.

"What the—Restrain that thing!"

As Matthew hunched forward, the Bigfoot's right hand slammed into the center of his chest, sending him off his feet. All the air in his lungs escaped and he swore he heard the sound of bone cracking under the weight of the blow. He landed on his backside some ten feet from where he had been standing.

"You all right?" asked Murphy.

"Not sure." Matthew tried to sit up, but a shockwave of pain coursed through him. *Definitely have at least one cracked rib.*

"You all right?" Murphy asked again as he took a step toward Matthew, leaving the log brace.

"Yeah. Never mind me. Keep doing what you're doing."

"You sure?" he asked.

"Hurry up, kid!" Nick cut in. "I'm almost through."

Murphy returned to his station and waited for the trunk to be sliced in two. The Bigfoot's whimpers turned into a constant bellow as it drummed its large hands against the tree trunk—its fear getting the better of it. From his current position, Matthew still saw the fear etched on the creature's face. He realized then that though the creature had shown gentleness and even some degree of reasoning, deep down it was still an animal.

The moment the chainsaw ripped through the tree trunk and Murphy applied the slightest pressure on the leveraged branch, the Bigfoot slammed its massive palms up and into the tree trunk. The tapering trunk hurled into the air and Murphy and Nick ducked down, allowing it to coast over their heads without injury.

In a flash, the creature leapt to its feet and gripped Nick's head in its hand.

"Get it off!" Nick demanded. He cut the chainsaw's motor off, an obvious attempt to calm the beast.

Murphy lunged to help, but was quickly swatted away with a backhand. His body soared into the air and landed close to Matthew, where he remained motionless. Matthew's gaze fixated on the young man, hoping to see a sign of life, but all he saw was a small trickle of blood run down the side of his face.

"Ahhh!" Nick screamed. Though his hands were barely able to circle the giant's wrist, they clung to it as tightly as they could. He kicked the beast, looking as though he was aiming for its groin, but he only managed to scrape its inner thigh.

"Hang on! I'm coming." Matthew tried to stand. Pain ignited his senses, but he clenched his teeth and pushed through it. His legs wobbled in protest, but he managed to get upright.

"Hurry! He's crushing my . . . ahhh!"

Blood jettisoned into the air through the creature's large, sausage-like fingers, the pressure applied to Nick's skull severe enough to break bone, split muscle, and pop veins. The Bigfoot brought Nick closer to itself and sniffed the air around him. With a grunt, the creature released its hold and Nick's body crumpled to the ground.

Matthew stared in horror at Nick's blood-soaked face. His friend and coworker of nearly ten years was unrecognizable with the fragments of his cheek bones pointing in different directions out of his face and brain matter oozing through the jagged tears in his skin.

Oh crap! he thought as the Bigfoot turned around and locked his gaze upon him.

"Ugh!" Murphy groaned as he positioned himself on all fours. "What happened?"

The Bigfoot roared and bounded toward the rookie.

"No!" Matthew said. "Leave him alone!"

"No . . . please!" Murphy pleaded as he struggled to get to his feet.

The Bigfoot stepped right up to Murphy and lumbered over him, not making a threatening move.

Murphy's body quivered as he tried to stand. Matthew couldn't tell if it was out of fear or from the backhanded blow. Tears streamed down from the rookie's wide eyes as he braced his hands against the creature's broad chest. With handfuls of auburn hair, he straightened his back and tilted his head upward to see the creature's face.

Afraid to make any sudden movements and spook the beast, Matthew stood and watched with unblinking eyes, praying the creature would just embrace its freedom and leave them alone.

"Please," Murphy begged as he released his grip on the Bigfoot's chest hair.

With a grunt, the creature whirl winded his arm and slammed his large fist into the top of Murphy's skull. Upon impact, his neck collapsed under the weight of the blow and his head sunk into his shoulders.

"Murphy!" Matthew stepped toward his friend to help. As the body dropped to its knees, he saw nothing but the whites of Murphy's eyes and knew there was nothing he could do. The rookie was lost.

"It's just us," he mumbled under his breath as the Bigfoot turned to face him once more. "Easy, boy!"

In a single bound the creature closed the gap between them, and with a speed beyond Matthew's comprehension, it grabbed hold of his throat and lifted him off his feet. The pressure on his windpipe made breathing near impossible.

"We were . . . only trying . . . to help."

The beast growled as it continued to squeeze. With its face contorted in a snarl, Matthew finally took notice of the two large eyeteeth and the two smaller canines in the lower mandibular arch. How he failed to recognize the creature as a meat eater, he did not know, but the fact was now staring at him.

His limbs went numb as his breaths became scarce.

Got to do something, he thought.

Using all the strength he could muster, he jabbed his thumb into the Bigfoot's eye. The creature released its hold and roared with displeasure as it stumbled back, rubbing the palm of its hand into the socket.

Matthew fell to his knees and took in a deep breath. He knew he needed to bolt out of there, but his body was too weak. His reaction time was off as unconsciousness threatened to take him.

By the time he turned around and took his first step away from the beast, he felt a pinch at his ankle, followed by sudden weightlessness. The world went topsy-turvy as he was lifted into the air.

This is it, he thought as he felt his body tug in the opposite direction.

The Bigfoot swung him round and slammed him into a nearby tree. The sound of bones cracking echoed in his ears as excruciating pain surged through his body, relaying he was still alive . . . for the moment.

The Bigfoot released him and he fell to the ground. He tried to move, but his body would not obey. Only his index finger managed to twitch in the damp soil.

My back, he thought, *it's broken.*

The creature bent forward and stared at him, and after a quick look-over, the Bigfoot started walking away.

An icy chill, colder than a winter night, enveloped Matthew's body. He watched the beast he thought he could have called a friend leave him helpless with no hope of rescue. Darkness crept over his field of vision, shrinking his line of sight.

Your secret will remain safe, he thought, *for now.*

The only comfort Matthew had in his final moments was the knowledge that once the authorities found him and the others dead, the woods would be scoured, and there would be no place for the nine-foot-tall giant to hide.

EVERGREEN SPRINGS

BY

JACK HESSEY

THE SMALL CLUSTER of cars and two lorries parked on the outskirts of the settlement was the first of many things that Lizzie found odd about the small town of Evergreen Springs.

She carefully eased her Volvo around a beat-up white pickup truck that was pulled up at the side of the road, twisting her head to the side to see what the cause for the collection of vehicles was.

Lizzie thought it was strange. Nobody seemed to have broken down, nobody seemed to have had an accident and it's not like the long, expanse of trees lining the side of the road were anything special; it was the same view that had greeted her for the past fifty miles or so. It just seemed to be a collection of men and women who had bizarrely pulled up outside of town to chug a few beers and have a chat.

She sighed and gave a shrug of her shoulders. She had seen weirder things in her cross-country journey across America to attend her parents' funeral up in Canada.

"Sweetie, we're getting close to a gas station?" Lizzie said, reaching behind her seat to give her snoozing, eight-year–old daughter's leg a quick shake.

Sandy rubbed her eyes and yawned. "Are we there yet?" she asked, blinking sleepily as she gazed out of the window.

Lizzie smiled; it was a question she had heard a dozen or more times on the journey. "Not yet," she replied. "We're just going to pull up for some gas, maybe get a burger for the road and so you can use the bathroom, okay?"

"What's that?" Sandy asked, completely ignoring Lizzie as she gazed out of the window, pointing her tiny hand at something to the left of her.

Lizzie eased her foot on the brake and glanced across to where her daughter pointed. "Creepy," she muttered under her breath as she gazed at the totem pole. "That's one ugly thing."

And it was ugly, too. Five-foot high and with a variety of ugly carvings of what seemed to be gorilla heads covering it, the only thing nice about it was the bouquet of red roses someone had left at the foot of the ugly thing.

"There's another one," Sandy said, pointing again.

Sure enough, there was another totem pole, identical to the first right down to the bouquet of roses at the bottom. In fact, the more Lizzie looked the more she realized there were more than two of the totem poles. As she pulled past a sign declaring WELCOME TO EVERGREEN SPRINGS she saw at least ten of them, each set the same distance apart and each identical to the last. They seemed to be ringing the town, almost as if they were some kind of guardians.

"Creepy," Lizzie said again, giving a small shudder as they pulled into the town itself.

Evergreen Springs was your typical small, American town. No more than a stop-off for cars travelling along the road through Uwharrie National Forest. A drug store, a tacky café and a gas station that doubled as a convenience store were the only commodities that she saw.

No sooner had she pulled up at the gas station than a fat, fussy old woman waddled over toward them. "Are you new in town?" she squawked from across the road, pausing to let a lorry pass by before crossing.

"Yes," Lizzie said as she clambered out of the car.

"Well, welcome to Evergreen Springs," she said, clasping her meaty hands together. "Alf! Alf! Why don't you come say hello?"

Alf slid out from underneath a beat-up, old BMW and turned out to be a stick-like old man with wispy gray hair. He walked toward them, wiping grimy hands on even grimier overalls as he did so.

"Don't get many strangers here," he said, looking especially curious at Sandy, who shrank away from his gaze.

"We're just passing through," Lizzie said firmly as she eased her way out of the car.

"Well, you folks go get yourself a bite to eat. I'll fill 'er up and check your oil." Alf said, flashing her a smile, which Lizzie couldn't help but find disturbing.

Still, she took Alf's advice and left the car in his hopefully capable hands as she went with Sandy to get something to eat.

The only place open was a small-but-clean-looking diner, staffed by a plump, red-faced man who gave them a friendly greeting and wasted no time in bringing them a couple of burgers and sodas.

"This is a weird town," Sandy said as she munched on her burger. "Everyone keeps staring."

Lizzie quickly glanced up and sure enough, the three other patrons at the diner, a trio of teenagers, were staring at them, smirking and giggling with each other.

"Just ignore them honey," Lizzie said, resisting the urge to give the three teens the finger.

A tap on her shoulder made her jump and Lizzie quickly spun around to face the round, beaming face of the restaurant manager.

"Fill your coffee up?" he said, giving the kettle in his hands a little shake.

Lizzie shook her head. They really needed to get going. Besides, she didn't like this town. There was something off-putting about it.

"Come now, I insist, it's on the house," the man said and, before she could stop him, the man filled up her mug. "And how about some ice cream for the little one?" he asked, turning his unsettling smile toward Sandy. Lizzie's daughter squirmed uncomfortably in her seat.

"No, we really must be off," Lizzie said firmly, rising to her feet. "Thank you for the offer, but we're in a rush."

Gripping her daughter tightly by the hand, she quickly led the way outside, trying her best to resist the urge to break out into a run and lock herself in her car.

When they arrived back at the car, Alf was hunched over the engine, working away at something.

At the sound of their approach he shot upright, a wrench clattering to the ground by his feet. "Just finished changing the oil, ma'am. Don't worry about paying for it. It was a pleasure, really."

Lizzie shook her head and forced the man to take the handful of bills she had removed from her purse. She always made sure to pay her own way in the world and wasn't going to accept freebies from anybody. Especially from strange, old men in odd little towns like this.

Lizzie had barely fastened her seatbelt on before she put her foot down. The quicker they put some miles between them and this place the better.

"Mom, those kids are hurting that old man!" Sandy suddenly said, her face pressed to the glass.

Lizzie eased on the break and glanced out the window.

On the street beside them, a hunched old man in a shabby overcoat shuffled his way down the road. Closely behind followed four nasty-looking teenagers who were hurling abuse, throwing tiny bits of gum at him and occasionally running up to give him a light slap on the back of the head.

Lizzie hesitated, the car moving at a crawl now. Was it worth getting involved? This didn't involve her, and there was no telling what the teens would do if she got bold and told them off. Besides, she had Sandy with her. There was no way she could risk helping the old man without risking her daughter's safety. What if the teens threw something at the car and hurt Sandy?

As Lizzie watched, one of the teens ran up and swiped at the plastic carrier bag the man had in his hand. The bag split and a pile of tin cans spilled onto the sidewalk.

That did it for her. No matter the risk, she wasn't going to sit by and watch this happen. She actually felt a little guilty for her past hesitation as she ground the car to a halt, unbuckled her seatbelt and got out of her car.

"Oi! Leave him alone," she shouted as loud as she could.

As one, the group of teens halted their torment of the old man and turned a nasty glare to her. For a few seconds—which seemed like an hour to Lizzie—they just stared and then, finally, one smirked.

"You're the chosen car!" he said loudly, raising his hand to point at them. For some reason this struck his friends as being very funny and they all fell about laughing.

Lizzie however, didn't get the joke. "Leave him alone," she repeated, taking a small step forward.

The teens laughed again, grinned and, much to Lizzie's relief, they walked off up the street.

"Thank you," the old man said gratefully as he scooped up his tin cans into his hands and shuffled toward them.

Lizzie blushed, suddenly feeling awkward. Before she could speak the man leaned close to her.

"Listen, you're a good person and I must tell you to . . ." he broke off at the sound of a door slamming shut and glanced fearfully over his shoulder.

"What's going on here?" a man in his thirties with the ruddy appearance of a trucker said.

"Nothing, nothing, I was just telling her directions is all," the old man said, lowering his head and shuffling off again.

The lie struck Lizzie as being a little odd, but she didn't mention it, supposing that perhaps the old man had reasons for it.

"Come on, Sandy," she said, shuddering a little as the trucker continued to stare at them. "Let's go."

They had only been driving for five minutes when the fog came in. Up until now it had been your typical, sunny August day, but the fog rolled in almost instantly, blanketing the ground and making it so Lizzie could barely see five feet in front of her.

"Mom, I don't like this," Sandy whispered from the backseat.

Lizzie turned to reassuringly smile at her daughter. "Don't worry, it's just fog. It's not gonna—"

Before she could finish the sentence there was a bang and the car lurched to the side. Lizzie slammed on the brakes and twisted the steering wheel to keep the car from plowing into the trees. They finally shuddered to a halt twenty feet down the road

"Mom, what happened?"

For once, Lizzie ignored her daughter as she turned the key in the ignition. It whirred, spluttered and failed to start. The engine was dead.

"Sandy, relax, it's just a minor fault, okay? I'll get out, take a look, and then if I can't fix it I'll call for help. We're not far away from Evergreen Springs. I'm sure someone will come out to help us."

She got out of the car and immediately shivered as the cold, clammy fog touched the bare flesh of her arms and legs. Lizzie immediately wished she had worn pants instead of a skirt and thought to pull a sweater on over her sleeveless blouse.

She popped the hood and gazed inside at the engine. It was a pretty pointless thing to do, she realized, suddenly feeling a bit stupid. What she knew about cars could be written on a postage stamp; there was no way she was going to fix the car by herself.

It was then that Lizzie heard the loud, braying call. It lasted a full thirty seconds and rose in volume the more it went on.

"Mom, what was that?" Sandy asked, winding the window down a crack.

"Nothing, it . . . it was just a bird," she said, trying and failing to keep her voice calm. Truth was, the noise had terrified her.

At that moment, another call answered it from the opposite side of the woods. Then another and another until the whole forest around them was alive with the long, braying calls that seemed like they were answering each other.

And then silence.

"Mom, get inside, I don't like it," Sandy said.

Lizzie didn't argue and quickly scrambled into the front seat. She slammed the door shut and made sure all the doors were locked before grabbing her cell phone.

"Don't worry, they're just birds," Lizzie said again. Despite her words, however, she had never heard a bird call like that. She wasn't an expert, but she had been on many hikes in the wilderness with her ex-husband and couldn't think of a bird call even remotely similar. Perhaps it was some animal? A moose or a deer, maybe?

That sounded much more likely, she decided. Just as she turned around to make this suggestion to Sandy, there arose a different call.

This one was a shrill giggle from the trees to the right of their car. Lizzie lifted her head, but couldn't make out a thing through the thick blanket of fog. As she tried to catch a glimpse of anything through the trees, another giggle sounded, this time from the left hand side of the car. This was followed up by a third, louder giggle that sounded like it was directly in front of them.

Even though Lizzie couldn't see properly, she got the feeling that whatever was making the noise was only a few feet away.

"Whoever is doing this go away. We're not scared," she shouted, dialing a number on her phone and pressing it to her ear.

She swore under her breath. No signal at all.

As she lifted the phone to dial a different number, the fog momentarily lifted, allowing her a view of the road in front of them.

There, for a split second, she saw a huge, looming figure with tree-trunk-like limbs bound away and into the cover of the fog.

"What was that?!" Sandy cried.

Lizzie winced. She'd been hoping her daughter hadn't seen whatever that thing was.

"Sandy . . ." she said softly, having no idea what to say. "Look, everything looks a lot scarier because of the fog. It's just some sort of animal, a moose or a deer or maybe a bear. It won't harm us, okay?"

Sandy looked like she was going to argue for a few seconds until she finally gave a small nod of her head.

"Brave girl," Lizzie said, giving her a warm smile.

By this point, the fog had closed in all around them again, blocking the road from view. No sooner had the fog resettled than a chorus of excited hoots and whistles broke out, the noises coming from all directions.

"They're not moose," Sandy said, giving a shake of her head. "Moose don't make noise like that."

Lizzie didn't reply; she listened intently, trying to get a picture of where the whistles were coming from.

The closest seemed to be coming from her right. She pressed her face against the glass, straining to see what was stalking them.

Stalking. Now that she thought the word, she couldn't shake it out of her mind. It was the perfect word to describe what was happening and, the more she thought about it the more she suspected that the creepy little town they had left knew something about whatever was lurking in these woods.

Now, thinking of the creatures lurking around the car as *things*, rather than animals like moose or deer, made her shudder.

All went silent. Lizzie couldn't shake the feeling the things were planning something.

"Mom, have they gone?" Sandy piped up from the backseat, her face pressed against the glass.

"I don't know," Lizzie said softly.

It had being ten minutes since the last howl, squeal, grunt, giggle or whistle.

Despite the silence, however, Lizzie didn't think the things would have left them that easily. With their whistles and hoots and giggles, she got the feeling the things were toying with her and she couldn't shake the sense this long silence was just another stage in the creatures' sick mind-games.

Just as the tension was starting to get to her, the fog cleared, just as quickly as it arrived.

Lizzie let out a piercing scream when she saw the creature staring into the car at her.

It was broad-shouldered, covered in shaggy, brown fur that covered its entire chest and face. The animal's face was apelike, long, with a jutting brow, sunken eyes and a large jaw, but its features were also more dexterous than any ape she'd ever seen.

The creature squatted on the floor next to the car with its face pressed directly against its window. How long it had been like that Lizzie had no idea, and even as she watched, the corners of the beast's mouth turned up into what was unmistakably a grin.

Try as she might, she couldn't pull her gaze away from the hideous creature.

Suddenly there came the sound of breaking glass, an angry howl and Sandy's scream from the backseat.

The sound of her daughter in peril was enough to shake Lizzie from her temporary paralysis, and she spun around.

At the other side of the car was another one of the creatures. This one had slammed a huge fist through the window and had gripped her daughter by the shirt with a pair of powerful hands.

Lizzie didn't hesitate. She flung her body in-between the two front seats, gripped her daughter's arm and pulled as hard as she could in an attempt to yank her out of the beast's grip.

Acting purely on instinct, she leaned forward and sank her teeth as hard as she could into the creature's wrist. It was like biting iron, such was the strength of the beast's skin. She gagged at the rank stench that poured up her nostrils and at the taste of the animal's damp fur.

The creature struck her on the top of her head with its free hand. Luckily, given the small space in the window, it couldn't get in much of a swing, but the blow was still hard enough to make Lizzie see stars.

"Get your hands off her!" Lizzie shouted above Sandy's scream, releasing her hold on the creature's arm to issue the threat before chomping down as hard as she could once more.

This time, instead of striking her, the creature heaved backwards in an attempt to drag both mother and daughter out of the car. At the same time, there was the sound of another window breaking and Lizzie viciously kicked out when she felt another pair of hands pawing at her feet. Her blind kick connected with a dull thud on the creature's face, but she might as well have being kicking a wall for all the good it did. "Mommm! Sandy cried, futilely clawing at the creature's arms as it slowly eased her out of the broken window.

CRACK!

The gunfire echoed around the forest, making Lizzie jump even mid-fight with the two monsters.

CRACK!

Lizzie heard a howl of pain before the grip on her ankles loosened, followed by a thud as the beast fell to the floor.

CRACK!

The third gunshot sounded and the creature attacking her daughter had had enough. It let out a howl of pain, released its hold on Sandy, and scampered off toward the trees where, Lizzie saw with a jolt of shock, were lined dozens more of the ape-like creatures.

Lizzie gave a quick shake of her head, stifling a shriek. She could worry about them later. Right now she had to check on her daughter.

"Sandy, are you all right?" she asked, wriggling through the gap between the two front seats to cradle her sobbing daughter in her arms.

Before her daughter could answer, the door behind Lizzie swung open. She spun around and cocked her fists, half-expecting to see the huge form of one of the ape-creatures staring in at her.

To her surprise, she found herself face-to-face with an old man. The same old man who she'd helped back in Evergreen Springs. He had a look of concern on his wrinkled face and had an old-fashioned rifle slung over his shoulders.

"You," she said, lowering her hands and blinking in surprise. "What are—?"

"No time," the man said with a wheeze. He did a quick glance behind him at the line of trees. "Come out, get in my car. Quick, we need to get out of here." Lizzie didn't need to be told twice. She was completely willing to put her safety in the hands of this old man if it meant getting herself and her daughter out of this forest and away from the ape-like creatures that lurked within.

Lizzie followed the old man to his car—an old Ford—and got in after him. She barely had time to make sure Sandy had fastened her seatbelt when the old man put his foot down on the accelerator.

"Okay," Lizzie said, still gazing out the window at the creatures, which had now lined the edge of the forest. There were at least over two dozen of them.

Each big, each powerful and each with rage-filled eyes. If this old man hadn't shown up to help then they would have been torn limb-from-limb.

"Okay," Lizzie said again, finally drawing her gaze away from the beasts to fix the old man with a hard stare. "What the hell is going on?"

The old man, who introduced himself as Old Petey, took a deep breath before explaining.

He explained that the creatures were Bigfoot and were extremely intelligent. The small town had been under siege for years until someone came up with the bright idea to offer a sacrifice to the animals. On the last day of every month at midday, the first person to pass through the town was offered to the group of Bigfoot. Any cars to be sacrificed were sabotaged at the gas station, set up so it broke down deep in the heart of Bigfoot territory.

The idea worked and the attacks on the town wore off. This tradition grew through the years to where the family of Bigfoot were honoured, and shrines were placed around the town to try and appease the animals.

The empty cars I passed on the way into town . . . Lizzie thought.

"I felt guilty," Old Petey said, slowing the car down now that he seemed to have judged to be a safe distance away from the town. "But I was too scared to do anything, scared that if I did, then they would end up sacrificing me to those monsters."

"What made you change your mind?" Lizzie asked, still glancing out of the window to see if any of the beasts were nearby.

"You did," Old Petey replied. "You helped me, showed me that people outside Evergreen Springs were good. You made me realize I needed to do something, and I think I came just in time."

Lizzie bit her lower lip and nodded before glancing over at her daughter. "It's okay, honey," she said softly, giving her a reassuring smile. "We're safe now."

THE GORGE

BY

BRYAN HALL

TANNER'S BREATH CAUGHT in his throat as the narrow trail opened up to reveal his goal. A half-mile away, the granite face of the Mummy Buttress glared at him. It was only the first stop on his week-long trip into the gorge, but it was the one he was most looking forward to.

Since taking up rock climbing four years earlier, he had made the trip to Linville Gorge at least once a year. Called "The Grand Canyon of the East" by many, the gorge was home to some of the best climbing on the East Coast. It was also incredibly wild. Even from the top of each ridge, with the ability to see for miles, no man-made structure was anywhere in sight.

The remoteness and wildness of the area was what had always appealed to him, Tanner supposed as he took a drink from his CamelBak. The weekend trips he'd made with his climbing partners never failed to fill him with a sense of calm, and never seemed to last long enough. The stresses of college always flooded back and drove out the fresh memories of nature that filled his soul when he was in the gorge. But graduation had been five days ago and he could think of no better way to celebrate earning his business management degree than by spending a week in the depths of the gorge. Heck, maybe even two weeks, depending on the fishing.

His plan was to hike the main ridgeline until it neared the Mummy Buttress, and then descend the twelve hundred or so feet into the gorge. From there, he planned on camping, climbing, fishing, and enjoying himself until his supplies dwindled to nothing. The plan, unfortunately, didn't appeal to any of his friends and he'd been forced to go it alone. Going solo on a climb wasn't a big deal, though, and he was ended up looking forward to the solitude.

Below him, the trail snaked down between the steep gorge walls. Three hundred or so feet below where he stood the tiny dirt path crossed a small waterfall before plunging straight down the embankment to the base of the gorge, close to the raging river that had carved the small canyon so many centuries ago.

Tanner shifted the weight of his pack and started down the trail, every few steps glancing at the cliff across from him and tracing the line he planned to climb as soon as he set up camp.

He reached the rim of the waterfall within a few minutes and paused, glancing over his shoulder. The feeling he was being watched crept over him, setting his skin tingling. He felt eyes on him, surveying his descent. He was sure of it. The sounds of animals, birds chirping and squirrels scurrying through the forest floor were amplified by the walls of the gorge and took on a kind of tinny ambience for a moment as he scanned the forest for anyone else who might be down here with him.

Shrugging off the sensation, Tanner stuck the CamelBak's hose in his mouth and took another drink of water.

While it was steep, the waterfall wasn't vertical by any means; it followed the slope of the gorge wall all the way down to the canyon floor, the stream continuing on and feeding into the river. About six feet wide, the ribbon of water bubbling over the granite it had long ago exposed seemed almost like a living thing. The sound of it alone was enough to make Tanner smile.

He gingerly stepped into the water, testing each foothold before taking the next step.

He'd crossed the stream several times before with no problems, but this time a thin layer of moss seemed to have formed over a portion of the granite underneath the flowing water.

He managed two steps across before realizing the moss was too slick. His foot slipped out from under him; he tried to lunge for the other side of the waterfall, but it was useless. He crashed onto his arm, a sickening pop accompanying a flash of pain that coursed the length of his arm, shoulder to fingertips.

Before his could even fully register the pain, he slid over the rim of the waterfall.

The fall seemed to last an eternity. He slid for most of the drop, like a kid riding one of the slides at a waterpark, but tumbling as he fell.

Within seconds the base of the gorge rushed up to meet him, and a surge of pain throughout his body sent him plunging into blackness.

He awoke in agony, his face half submerged in the stream. He lay still for a moment, trying to bring his jumbled thoughts into focus. His shorts and shirt were soaked and cold. The pain in his right leg was the worst, a searing white-knuckled bastard that made it hard to concentrate on anything else. He knew without trying to move it that his left arm had been broken; he'd known that before he'd even pitched over the edge of the waterfall. His left ankle screamed out as well, throbbing and tight against his soaking wet hiking boot. There were other little pains, too. Burning scrapes and scratches stung all over his body, but they were insignificant compared to the agony beneath his skin.

With his good arm, he forced his body onto its side and then fumbled with the backpack's straps, undoing them. Every movement he made sent pains churning through his limbs, but after a few terrible moments he managed to shrug off the pack.

Free from the heavy pack, Tanner propped himself on his elbow and checked his leg. Just below his knee, his leg had turned blue and black and was swollen to twice its normal size. The leg itself awkwardly to one side, twisting out at an unnatural angle where the bone had snapped. The swelling in his left ankle was immense as well, and even through his sock he could tell the break was severe.

Tanner saw movement in his peripheral vision. He snapped his head upwards, expecting a fisherman or hiker to be rushing to his rescue.

A hundred or so feet from him, near the river's edge, was an animal unlike any he'd ever seen before. It was half-obscured by the underbrush, but what he could see chilled his blood.

It was a man—or, at least, it resembled one. Thick, dark hair hung in matted clumps from its head, and much of its face was covered by a thick beard. The parts of its body that were visible were hairy as well, covered in a pelt that made it look almost like an ape. But its face . . . its face was far too human for an ape, even from such a far distance. It was large as well, at least as big as a man but much stockier. The creature stared at him, unmoving. If he hadn't noticed its approach it would have nearly blended in with the forest around it.

Tanner couldn't move. The pain still enveloped him like a blanket, but aching fear paralyzed him. His eyes were fixed on the creature, watching it watch him.

It jerked its head once, then a second time, as if shaking off some bug or pest that he couldn't see. Then, slowly, it began to move along the riverbank, stepping sideways while it kept its eyes locked on him. Within a moment, it was out of sight.

Tanner stared at the forest, watching the spot the creature had disappeared from and tried to process what he'd seen.

A bear.

That was his first thought. The gorge was home to countless animals, black bears included. And it was the time of year where they would likely be hunting for food. The thing had been large enough for a bear, that was certain.

Yet it had walked upright, its sideways stride taken with long, sure steps.

And its face had been so familiar, so human. Of course he'd been knocked out cold in the fall, and the animal had been a good distance from him, his mind easily could have been playing tricks on him, conjuring up features that weren't there.

His injuries pulled his mind from the beast. As his head slowly recovered from the after-fog from his fall, the intensity of his pain was steadily increasing. He shifted his weight on his arm, pulling himself forwards a few inches and sent lightning bolts of agony up his legs. He cried out softly, surprised by how much it hurt to simply move.

Tanner gritted his teeth and pulled himself along again, moving another few inches. He continued that way, a hushed cry of pain punctuating each movement until he was finally out of the stream, laying on his back and struggling to catch his breath.

A howl sliced through the forest, locking his labored breaths in his chest as it echoed off the canyon walls and creating an ungodly choir. Starting as a high-pitched wail and slowly descending through a dozen octaves, it sounded somewhat similar to a coyote's cry but with a deeper timbre and something unmistakably alien laced within it.

The last vestiges of the cry slowly stopped reverberating off the gorge's rock faces and gave way to chirping birds and screeching squirrels.

Tanner tried to place the strange sound with a source but couldn't. Nothing he'd ever heard in the wild sounded like what entered his ears just now, and he knew that his mind hadn't conjured up the cry. Something was in the woods with him, and he had no clue if it was aggressive or not. If it was dangerous, he couldn't defend himself from it or even run away.

Tanner gave in to his fears and screamed into the pristine blue sky above him. "Help! Somebody help me!"

His own voice was the only response, bouncing from mountainside to mountainside like the wail of a ghost.

It was Wednesday. The gorge saw the majority of its visitors over the weekend since the remote nature of it made it unpopular for midweek trip, but there was always the chance someone was out hiking or climbing or fishing. *He* was, after all.

Tanner screamed again, begging for help. His screams turned to sobs for a brief second, but he pushed self-pity out of his mind. He'd read enough and heard enough climbing stories to know the only way to survive a situation like the one he was trapped in was to remain calm.

The only option was to carry on as he had been, dragging himself out of the gorge. It sounded impossible given the incredibly steep ascent leading back up to the main trail. The two feet he'd moved out of the stream had seemed like a mile, and now he faced two *actual* miles back to the parking lot. Still, he had little choice but to do it.

Grimacing, he rolled back onto his side and began to pull himself through the underbrush inch by agonizing inch, moving toward the area where the trail led down from the waterfall to the base of the gorge.

He tried to focus on his car—his only chance at survival. Keeping his mind on it helped block out some of the pain, to help drive him forward through the agony. After what seemed like hours he'd managed forty or so excruciating feet through the briars and mountain laurel, the edge of the trail in view another twenty feet above him, when he heard something large move in the forest behind him.

He froze, listening.

Dry leaves crunched underneath something heavy and a grunting drifted up the slope almost like a wild boar snorting as it rooted for food. Cracking, snapping and the sounds of something ripping joined the noise.

Tanner forced himself to look over his shoulder.

The animal squatted over his backpack, tearing it to shreds and sifting through the contents. He could see it more clearly now. A jolt of panic shot through his body and for a moment his mind went blank.

To his surprise, he discovered his addled mind hadn't invented anything at all; the animal was definitely not a bear. It looked like a massive man, even larger than the pro wrestlers his old college roommate used to be obsessed with. Its legs were as thick as small trees, its arms not much smaller. The entirety of its body was covered in thick hair, black in some patches, brown in others. The long, matted dreadlocks swung from side-to-side as it tore through his pack.

The thing thrust Tanner's extra clothing to its face in fistfuls, snorting and sniffing them before tossing them to the side. As it found the dehydrated food and crackers Tanner had packed it greedily crammed them into it mouth. Although it was only one beast, it sounded like a dozen creatures feasting simultaneously.

He'd never believed in it before, but seeing it so closely, Tanner knew immediately what the beast was.

Watching the animal, Tanner continued to drag himself up the hill. If he could reach the trail, he might be able to move out of the creature's sight. It didn't guarantee safety at all, but to be out of sight would at least ease his mind somewhat.

At least, he told himself so.

Fear and adrenaline numbing his pain and driving him forward, he managed to move another ten or so feet when the creature finished rifling through his backpack. It ripped the canvas from the metal frame and threw both to the ground, then looked directly up the bank and locked eyes with Tanner. A beard covered much of its face, although the hair wasn't as thick as that which covered its body. A steep sloping forehead and sunken eyes sat above a broad, flat nose.

The creature took a few steps toward him, grunting louder and louder as it did.

Tanner glanced around, frantically trying to find something to defend himself with—a branch he could use as a club, a rock, anything!

A softball-sized stone lay a few feet above him; he pulled himself toward it. It was within reach in seconds and he grabbed it and rolled to his back, forcing himself to sit upwards through his pain.

Below him, the creature stood still and silent, staring up at him with its head cocked to one side like a curious puppy regarding some new wondrous discovery.

They stared at one another for a moment like gunfighters about to draw until the animal took two quick steps up the bank. It managed a third and Tanner lobbed the rock at it, connecting with its hulking shoulder.

The beast unleashed a hellish cry, animalistic but unmistakably filled with pain, shock and anger. It stumbled backwards then turned and thundered down the bank, vanishing into the forest again with only its screams and Tanner's destroyed pack as evidence it had even been there.

Tanner watched the forest until he was certain the creature had fled then returned his attention to reaching the trail above. The pains in his legs and arm were massive, but the sheer adrenaline of his encounter seemed to have lessened the agony somewhat and he covered the last dozen feet within moments, pulling himself off the slope onto the trail. While the trail was still steep, it was nowhere near as steep or rough as the hill he'd just managed to climb, and his confidence was gaining that he could actually make it back to the parking lot. It would be hell, the upcoming crawl, but despite the distance it would be nothing compared to what he'd just done.

He began to pull himself up the narrow dirt trail, stopping every few minutes to catch his breath and scan the forest for any sign of the beast he seemed to have chased off. It took ages for him to reach the waterfall that had begun his ordeal, and Tanner paused at the edge of it to peer over the edge at the gorge below. His demolished backpack seemed tiny from where he now was, a testament to how far he'd managed to crawl.

His nerves steeled, he was about to drag himself across the top of the waterfall when he saw movement in the woods below.

It was back.

It moved out of the trees to where his torn pack lay, then stood there looking about the forest. Tanner moved his head back until he could just barely see over edge of the trail, confident the creature below couldn't see him.

A moment passed and the beast dropped to its knees and put its face to the ground.

Smelling, Tanner thought. *The stupid thing's trying to smell me.*

The creature raised its head and pulled itself up to a squat and looked around. A series of grunts echoed through the canyon, and the beast threw its head back, unleashing another of its blood-curdling screams.

Tanner watched with horror as the massive animal leaped over the stream and started to move up the hillside, following the same path he'd taken while dragging himself up the trail not too long ago.

Panic began to replace his confidence and he pulled himself back into the cold mountain water. His elbow slipped out from beneath him and he thought for an instant he would pitch over the waterfall's edge again, but he didn't.

He was across it in seconds, rushing to drag himself up the trail.

It was behind him.

Tracking him.

Stalking him.

Hunting him.

Tanner tried to rise onto all fours so he could move faster, but the pain was a blinding hell and he collapsed to his stomach with a cry. There was no time to wallow in his agony, however, and he immediately resumed his slow crawl up the trail. Every few feet he glanced over his shoulder, each time expecting to see the beast bearing down upon him and each time seeing nothing but the pitiful track his body left in the dirt.

He reached the point where the trail into the base of the gorge reached the main path and looked behind him again. The animal was slowly moving up the trail behind him, still a good distance away. It stopped every few steps to sniff the ground again as if unsure it was actually on the right path.

Tanner continued on for another twenty feet and stopped, panting.

There was no way he could outrun it. Even though it constantly stopped to check for his scent, it was still moving faster than his destroyed body could ever hope to.

He rolled off the trail and through the woods until he was on the edge of another steep slope, ten feet or so from the trail. He started to scoop out the dead leaves from in front of him, digging a hole to the forest floor. When he reached the earth beneath the leaves, he climbed into the hole and frantically pulled the leaves over himself. Within moments, he was completely buried beneath them save for a small opening he'd left so he could watch the trail.

Tanner didn't have to wait long; the creature was closer to him than he'd thought and felt its approach seconds before it bounded into his view, its heavy footsteps reverberating through the ground beneath him.

It stopped in the trail directly in front of him and dropped to its knees again, sniffing the ground with the loud snorting of a hog. Ten feet from the beast, Tanner fought the urge to gag as the air filled with a pungent, musky smell so thick and rich it made his eyes water.

The creature quickly looked around then continued down the trail, stopping after another fifteen or twenty feet.

Tanner could barely see the beast as it dropped to the ground and tried to locate his scent.

It stood and turned back, its jaw hanging slack and showing massive black teeth.

The creature returned to the spot he had left the trail and cried out, its scream deafening at such a close proximity. It sniffed the ground again and instantly left the trail, heading directly toward him.

Tanner burst out of his makeshift grave, frantically clawing his way across the forest floor.

The creature unleashed a long, guttural growl as it pressed down upon him. He felt its breath on his bare legs as he reached the edge of the slope and knew he had little choice.

Without hesitation, he threw himself off the edge of the ridge and allowed his body to go limp as it tumbled down the steep mountainside, pitching back down another section of the gorge.

His leg slammed into a tree, whatever hadn't broken before now completing shattering. Then his side, connecting with some unseen obstacle, cracking his ribs with a sickening snap.

He fell for what seemed like miles, his body slowing as the slope of the gorge lessened until finally he came to rest in a tangled mass of briars and rhododendron. There was no unconsciousness this time, no reprieve from the pain or fear.

Tanner lay still, crying softly while he stared at the exposed bone that had torn its way through the skin of his leg, a bleached-white alien trying to escape from his mangled body. Shaking all over, panic setting his heart into overdrive, he squeezed his eyes shut.

More vibrations in the ground.

He opened his eyes. The creature made its way down the gorge, amazingly nimble for its huge size. It used the trees to navigate its descent, grabbing saplings and swinging from one to the next as it pursued him.

As it reached the bottom, it cried out in its ungodly voice again.

From behind Tanner, a response came. The second howl was more high-pitched than the first, and was followed by a third, weaker cry. Then, from farther away, another scream.

Tanner tried to look behind him but couldn't see the source of the howling.

He didn't need to.

As the creatures' footsteps surrounded him, he tried to focus on the pain that consumed his broken body.

Somehow, it seemed better than thinking of what was to come.

GO TOWARD THE LIGHT

BY

LARRY BERRETH

THE FIRST THING Jonas saw that night was the hairy brown appendage creeping over the edge of his property. At the time he thought it was just some mangy coyote, retreating after making a play for Maxie.

He was a tough little bastard, much like Jonas Gostavson himself. Loud, stubborn, and never one to run from a scrap with someone bigger, Maxie had more in common with his owner than Jonas would ever agree.

Jonas hadn't always been the nicest of fellows, but according to the old adage, didn't nice guys finish last.

He only stood about five-five, but with his blustery manner and determination, he was a Napoleon among men.

He stood up to his abusive father at age fourteen, putting himself between him and his long suffering mother, driving the drunken loser from their home. He hadn't seen the old man in over thirty years, and hadn't missed him for a minute.

He worked his way through college, started his own independent hardware store, and eventually opened two more despite interference from a couple national chains.

He won over his high school sweetheart, sired a son, and although they had their differences—what kind of a man forsakes the family business to major in "creative writing"? —he even persuaded the boy and his gold-digging daughter-in-law to finally come visit him this Christmas.

He hadn't seen his only grandchild since just after her birth. She was four years old now and had no real memory of him. But that would change.

They had never come to visit him before at Christmas, even after the cancer had claimed Susan.

Part out of spite, part out of wanting to put on a big show for his little Marigold, he had put up thousands of lights, enough to illuminate the whole valley. He ordered the best and brightest he could find, even shipping in old traditional style blow molds of Santa, Frosty, and all the reindeer from the store's catalog for the front yard.

Chevy Chase would be proud, he thought, sharing a splash of his beer into Maxie's bowl.

He wasn't that crazy about the little dachshund at first, but it was Susan's darling. After she passed, he proved to be a loyal companion, and perhaps his only real friend.

Wild fires had ravaged rural Boulder County that summer. Even after the evacuation order, he and Maxie had stayed. So what if his constant unauthorized use of the hose and sprinklers to protect his property had affected the water pressure in his neighborhood? His property still stood. If the others had really cared, they would have stayed also.

The fires had come one after another that summer. Some were caused by lightning, some by careless human error. There had been reports of wildlife venturing closer, braving the mountain mansions in search of food. There had even been reports of mischievous bears down in suburban Denver that Fall.

Maxie had been especially hyper the last few days. He patrolled the western edge of the lawn, just past the swimming pool, obsessively marking the edge where it dropped into the ravine. Jonas thought the little guy was developing a bladder condition. He even entertained thoughts of the little hairball catching a social disease from the shitzu in the cul-de-sac down the street.

He was frying some ground round for their dinner when he heard Maxie barking. Usually it sounded more like hoarse squeaking, but this time it was preceded by gruff snarling and urgency.

He pushed the frying pan to the back burner and went to the glass door.

A large, shaggy monstrosity, silhouetted in the setting twilight, bounded over the drop from the gulch, raising a massive arm to strike at Maxie.

Jonas flicked on the Christmas lights and threw up the sliding glass door as the beast started its downswing.

All involved parties were momentarily blinded.

The little dog leapt back, its paws folding underneath, and almost fell in the pool.

Jonas immediately thought it was an invading bear, but as he fought the light flecks to fade from his eyes he thought he saw an almost human face.

One full of desperation and anger.

The creature let out a curdling bellow, throwing its arm in front of its face and, turning, jumped back down into the gulley below in one quick motion.

Maxie shot between his legs. He bounced off the kitchen bar, releasing a splash of urine upon impact, and ricocheted into Jonas's bedroom and under the bed.

Jonas ran the couple steps back inside and slammed the glass door shut. He pulled the curtain across to cover it, and took a couple steps back. He didn't have any actual experience with bears, and he had never seen one on the Nature Channel that made a sound like that or seemed that agile.

The phone rang. His heart tried to escape his ribcage. He grabbed his chest and caught his breath. "Get a hold of yourself, old man," he whispered, forcing his breathing to slow. By the fourth ring, he was able to drag himself over to the wall phone and answer. Hello?" he grunted.

"Dad? It's Ernie." His son's voice was upbeat but distorted by the poor cellular transmission. "Are you okay? You sound weird."

Jonas pressed the phone to his ear and cautiously moved the curtain aside to peer out. Everything looked clear.

"I'm all right. I was just startled by the phone."

"We're pretty worn out from the drive, but Mari's real excited to see her grandpa."

Who was Ernie kidding? He was the one doing all the driving. Based on the pictures he had seen the last couple years, Christine was probably sitting back looking at fashion magazines, choosing this week's hair color.

"I think we're just going to press on. We should be there in a couple hours," Ernie said.

Jonas looked toward the whimpering sounds in his bedroom then out to the backyard again.

He hadn't seen Ernest since Susan's funeral, and little Mari needed to see him as much as he needed to see her, or at least that's what he told himself.

Nothing was going to stand in the way of this visit.

"I'll be ready," Jonas said. "Just honk your horn when you pull in, in case I'm asleep."

"Won't that wake the neighbors?"

"They can go to hell."

Jonas hung up.

He cleaned up the little dog's nervous mess, both by the kitchen and in his bedroom. It took the evening's burnt hamburger to coax Maxie out from under the bed and stop his shaking.

Jonas thought about calling the sheriff's department about the bear. He mulled over the look of hatred in its crinkled bald face and piercing eyes. It had to be a bear. What else could it be? Ultimately he decided against calling the authorities. After all, they wouldn't be in any big hurry to drive all the way out there to look for an animal on Christmas Eve. Damned liberal Boulder sheriff would probably write him a ticket for harassing the wildlife. He also didn't want Ernie and his family pulling in the long driveway to find flashing red and blue lights.

He would handle this matter himself.

Preparation was usually key, but he didn't have much time before they arrived. Jonas marched to the garage to retrieve his old deer hunting rifle. It had been years since he last used it, but the gun had remained dust free in the cabinet he'd built for it. He fumbled briefly with the key for the lock, but his hand steadied once he grasped its smooth walnut stock. He examined its parts, and deemed it good for a quick outing. He pulled back on the bolt, and racked in as much ammo as he could. Jonas even stuffed a couple spare shells in his sweater pocket.

Next, he went to the kitchen and patted the leftover hamburger into a couple of large greasy meatballs. He even warmed them up a bit to make them a more enticing bait, much to Maxie's delight and disappointment.

Jonas coaxed Maxie back into the bedroom and closed the door behind the sneaky dog.

He gathered up his supplies and took up position in his dinner chair, just inside the backyard door. Jonas killed all the lights, and waited until Maxie stopped protesting. After what he deemed to be a couple quiet minutes, he slowly eased the glass door open and underhand tossed the two meatballs near the end of his property. They were just far enough from the edge that whatever wanted them would not be able to scoop them up and have to move within his gun sight.

Jonas sat back and relaxed the weapon across his legs, allowing his eyes to adjust to the dark. He heard Maxie scratching at the door and hoped he'd settle down and be quiet. The scuffing soon stopped, and Jonas returned his attention to the faint meatballs on his lawn on Christmas Eve.

The evening breeze helped move some clouds across the moon. Jonas thought he saw something near the tip of the lawn. He was about to dismiss it as a shadow, when it started to grow in size.

He secured his grip on the rifle and raised it.

The uncertain bulk was almost at the first meatball.

Maxie darted through his chair legs toward the midnight snack. Jonas jumped up, swearing, and ran outside after him. He hit the lights on as he stumbled through the door. He was about halfway between the house and the closest meatball when Maxie snatched it in his tiny jaws and veered to the left, running to the far side of the pool.

A growing rumble came from the area of the furthest meatball as the indistinct shape grew, standing up to its full height. The thing looked like a cross between a brown bear and a gorilla, with enormous feet and hands. It must have been an easy eight feet, Jonas surmised.

And it was moving in his direction.

Jonas braced himself for the recoil, and fired from the hip, directly into the snarling abomination's core as it bore down on him. It stopped for a second, as though kicked in the gut, but no blood or flesh expelled from it. He fired again, but the second round did not have any better success against its tough, muscular hide.

The beast started toward him.

The hunting rifle barely made a dent. What else could he do?

He flashed on the thought of throwing it at the creature like the crooks did in the old *Superman* show. He realized that would be equally futile and instead raised it like a club, waving it around, cursing.

The hairy behemoth trudged closer, straddling the space between the deck and the pool. Each ungodly footstep shook his recently-decorated deck and rattled its lights.

Jonas swung the rifle at it. The huge fingers of the beast's left hand grabbed the butt, halting it in midair. Jonas felt like he had hit a brick wall with an aluminum baseball bat as the sudden stop vibrated through his forearms.

The savage brute squeezed, crushing the rifle stock into powder and crumbs. It threw back its head and the fanged, slobbering maw released a maniacal howl. It casually dropped what was left of the weapon. Swiftly, it raised its trunk-like right arm to swat at Jonas, but caught it in the strand of Christmas lights lining the top of the deck. It looked up at the blinking lights around its hand, confused. The beast jerked its arm down, ripping the line of lights and adding to the tangle around its wrist.

Maxie leapt at it from behind, yipping and trying to get a secure bite on the scraggly, matted fur of the creature's calf.

Jonas gaped at the light-entangled monstrosity. Time froze for one ridiculous, horrible instant as the wild missing link was distracted by the *pop* and *crunch* of C9 bulbs, the annoyance of Maxie's battle barks, and the shine of the multi-colored lights.

Seeing it bend toward Maxie, Jonas returned to the moment and grabbed the nearest patio chair, slamming its metal frame across the invader's jaw as hard as he could. The creature looked not so much hurt as offended. It raised its leg, hesitating between crushing the nipping nuisance and stepping toward the tiny man.

Jonas seized what might be his last opportunity and shoved the legs of the chair into the monster's mangy throat and face. He heaved as best he could, ducking a final swipe of its massive left arm as he managed to knock the beast off balance in midstep and into the pool.

The small swimming pool was only nine feet deep, but the invader fell into its deepest end. Its weight drew it immediately to the bottom, with its shaggy head still only about a foot from the surface.

The giant madly thrashed as electricity from the commercial grade light cord arced into the water. Sparks flew from the top of the pool as all the lights in the home flickered on and off. Random crackles, pops, and hisses accompanied the light show with the growing stench of smoke from somewhere in the house and burning hair.

Even underwater, the creature's garbled shriek could be heard with equal parts desperation and rage.

The power from the house finally gave out, and so did the struggling beast.

As the churning water settled, the burned-out light strand snapped, landing inches from Maxie's snout. The little dog decided he had enough, too. He let out one quick yelp, then ran past his owner back into the house.

Jonas, who had landed hard on his backside, unshielded his eyes and furiously blinked against the residual optic fireworks that disrupted his vision. He cautiously listened for any movement from the beast, but the only activity from the pool was the settling sloshing. He crawled to the edge of the water and peered over.

Splayed long hair buoyed in the water above the immense dark form. It was limp and unmoving, except for the residual waves.

This would be a heck of a story to tell the grandkids flitted through his mind. He rolled over on the ground, laughing in relief.

He eventually wiped the tears from his eyes and forced himself to his knees, taking one more look at his nightmare. Its body remained motionless as it slightly bobbed in the water.

Still chuckling, Jonas pushed on his knees to stand and turned toward the demolished Christmas lights.

The last thing he heard was a horn beep twice and a car door slam.

Something sprang from the water's surface and clamped around his ankle. It yanked him down with tremendous speed. His chin smacked the edge of the pool and he felt some of his teeth shattered as he entered the water.

The last thing he saw was the shadowy hulk as it hurtled upward past him, and he sank further into the water.

THE BEAST-MEN OF THE GREAT VALLEY

BY

J.W. SCHNARR

For as long as can be remembered, our people have walked the lands between the hills at the foot of the mountains, where plains stretch out like a long yellow blanket as far as the eye can see. When sun brings warmth and the herds come out of the hills, we follow them north and food is bountiful. When the snows come, we head south where the wind has fewer teeth and the woolly mammoth stalks the plains.

It is known to our people the edges of things in this world are also edges in other worlds; that places where the plains overlap the hills are also places where the lands of the dead and the living overlap.

We have been tasked to walk those lands and remain vigilant, and we are proud to do so because we are the strongest and wisest of all the hill peoples, and we are the fastest and cleverest of all the plains peoples.

But as clever and wise and fast and strong as we are, few ever suspected that in the place where the hills and plains meet and the living and the dead connect there might be another land that appears from time to time, a land of things that were *never meant to be*—a place of monsters so horrid that to gaze upon them is to give birth to a seed of terror in your heart that will take root in your dreams and bear nightmares as fruit.

It is those same monsters of which our people are now speaking, whispering from stuttering mouth to fevered ear. I do nothing to calm their worries. Instead, I tell them how The Great Owl has vomited his hell-spawned pellets upon the earth and birthed the monsters that plague the hills like locusts. I tell them they have every right to fear the orange blazes in the hills and the inhuman drumming that accompanies them. I have seen the beast-men of the Great Valley, and am afraid.

Those who know me know I was an able warrior before my hands were ruined, a hunter matched by few others, and with my war axe none were better. I fought with my head and defended the tribe with my heart.

I might have been the best were it not for my rivalry with Mok, who was a year older and somewhat taller than I, and in all things my equal. But if I am honest with myself I must admit he was actually my better in many things and it is only my sinking pride that allows me to say it now.

But there was a time when to utter such words to me brought about great rage and violence.

On one such day I was with Mok, chasing deer into the hills along with our tribal brothers, and we numbered twenty or so. We'd already bagged enough meat for the tribe when I spotted a prize buck upon a rock some ways away. The creature was surely a gift to the tribe; it was taller and fatter than any animal I'd ever seen, with a long, wide rack upon its head like a mighty crown.

Mok picked a handful of men from our party to chase down the beast, slapping me on the back as he passed. Of course I would be among those who hunted the buck; it had been my keen eyes that had spotted it first. Such was my right. I daresay I wasn't going to let Mok hunt it down for his own glory. I intended to down the animal myself.

We headed into the hills, fleet of foot and dancing on the wind as only our tribe knows how, pushing through the grasses and trees silent as ghosts with only the occasional rustle of grass to mark our passing. The buck caught wind of malice in the air and turned on a heel deeper into the hills. If it was to be a gift from our gods, it was to be a gift we must earn, and only when a gift is earned is a gift truly deserved.

As we crested a hill I saw the buck eating grass some ways away, and I grabbed up my bow and let loose a bronze-headed arrow and struck true in the beast's neck. 'Twas surely a killing blow, but the beast staggered and then fled west toward the mountains. It bled and bled, and we were able to pick up the scent of it in the trail it left behind.

Mok and I ran far ahead of the others, as we both wanted to grant the buck its killing blow. I had wounded it, true, but real glory in the eyes of the tribe was reserved for he who brought it down. Many times had meat been lost after suffering an injury, simply wandering off into the clutches of the forest never to be seen again. I did not want that to happen almost as much as I did not want Mok to fell the creature first, although in my prideful, secret heart I knew I would rather lose the meat for the tribe than have Mok loured his kill over me. Such is the pride of youth.

We trailed the buck for hours, always catching a glimpse of it here, or a snatch of movement there, but always keeping true to the course by the line of blood in the dirt, or on leaves and branches of the trees and bushes it passed.

As the sun finished its race in the west, our little group gathered to discuss what was to be done. Twilight was washing in and our people know that is a time when a man's senses could not always be trusted.

Sound carries foul in the air, and your eyes can play tricks on you in the grim half-light. It is this time between darkness and light when many hunters are injured. The spirits delight in assaulting us with hidden logs and stones meant to trip and scrape. Knowing this, several of our men thought it wise to head back. We had caught our fill for the day. There was feasting and drinking and other carnal pleasures awaiting us back at the camp.

Mok looked at me, though, and I knew we were only going further into the hills. He didn't have to question my manhood with his words to get me to agree to this. Such was my need to outdo him that a mere glance to see if I wanted to continue on or not was all that was needed. By the gods, I *did*.

So we set off into the gloom, following the buck deep into the hills, further than even Mok or I had gone before, for hours, in the dark, following the scent of blood on the ground. Eventually we came upon a deep basin surrounded and filled with trees of a type we'd never seen before, like the rustic pines on the hills but twisted and moody from the strange winds that blew, and dusted grey as though the skies had bled fine ash instead of snow. In the bottom of the basin we saw the orange glow of a large fire and heard the beating of many drums like powerful heartbeats ringing through the valley.

We were all of us afraid, except for Mok, and he laughed in my face when I suggested we let the buck go and return to familiar lands. He called me a coward and I might have fought him there for his biting tongue were it not for the fact one of the others spotted the buck, now weak from blood loss, staggering along a rocky path down the valley and below us.

We moved on the creature as one then, and I did my best to push the drumbeats from my head. We fanned out in a half circle, a common trap for a small group of men hunting a large animal. As we moved in for the final kill, however, there was a crash in the woods in front of the buck that sent him scurrying toward us. He hadn't gone far when a single large stone sailed from the trees and crushed its skull. I'd never seen such an accurate throw with so large a stone. The buck staggered and fell to the ground dead before us.

The trees erupted with whooping and chanting, and when they parted I saw a creature straight out of a nightmare. I swear to the gods I would have fled the moment they came out of the whispering dark if fear had not made my feet numb and cold.

There were three of them, a-man-and-a-half tall with hulking upper bodies and long muscled legs. They walked like men but also beastlike; it reminded me of how the great bears would sometimes stagger about on two legs. These creatures were not bears, however, and I could tell from their shape they were meant to walk upright as we do. They were broad-shouldered and carried great strength; the size of their arms easily matched the size of a man's leg. But the most terrible feature of these beast-men was the long, knotted and filthy hair that covered their bodies from head to foot as though they were a mating of the great cave bears of old and men. As long as I've lived I have never once heard of such a thing happening, and I have lived a long time.

The three beast-men carried stone spears, not unlike other primitive mountain tribes our people conquered in the past, but these spears were longer and thicker than any I'd ever seen a man carry. They wore no clothing save for a leather strap that wound over one shoulder and around their waists; there were items hanging from those belts I couldn't make out in the dark.

The beast-men thumped their chests and jostled each other as brothers while they approached their prize. Then, kneeling before the buck, they turned on it with their bare hands, rending hot flesh from the body and feasting on its organs. Surely no man had ever set upon a creature with such ferocity. Again I was reminded of a bear. One of the creatures pulled my arrow from the buck's shoulder and snapped it cleanly in half, tossing it to the side.

Mok was furious. He started to move on the creatures and I grabbed him by the arm.

"That's our meat," he hissed through clenched teeth.

"Let's leave this place," I begged. It was a mistake, for the only thing Mok hated more than being beaten for game was a show of weakness.

He pulled away from me, eyes blazing in the dark. "Be a coward," he whispered, "but go somewhere else to do it." With that he drew a bronze arrow from the quiver at his hip and stalked off toward the beasts.

I had no choice but to follow, and the others had an equal amount of choice but to follow me. We moved again as ghosts until we were just a short distance from the beast-men. They were focused only on their meal, feasting with abandon and making noise like they truly had none to fear in the forest. I believed that to be true, because I was terrified of them.

They were even larger up close, giants by our standards. The yellow-haired dragon men of the north are said to have giants among them, but these beasts would dwarf even those yellow demons.

Mok, if he was scared, refused to show it. He notched his arrow then stood and fired it directly into the flank of the closest beast.

That was our sign that the battle was on. The creatures howled like old forest wolves and sprang to their feet, casting the body of the buck aside as an afterthought. The others threw the deer carcass aside and did the same. They took their sapling spears in hand and charged toward Mok, who was whooping and notching another arrow. To our credit, we raised our bronze-spiked war clubs and rushed to meet them in open combat as fearless men would, although we were all terrified.

What fierceness the beast-men possessed! They fought in a rudimentary but effective style, swinging and thrusting their great spears with precision brought on by brute strength. They howled continuously while they fought, and the stench of their bodies added to the power they held over us. Closing on them to take advantage of our speed caused us to gag and wretch at the stink, like waste and blood and sweat in a mix I had never dreamed possible

A beast-man took one of our warriors in his hands and lifted him high off the ground before folding the man back on himself and forcing his severed spine to push through his belly. The man's screams died in his throat as gurgles of blood with his last breath. The beast cast the man aside like a broken toy then set upon another. It failed to see Mok and his deadly bow, however, and before the beast had taken more than a handful of steps Mok had buried two arrows in its chest.

I would have seen more but I was set upon by my own beast-man. He approached cautiously, ever circling while testing my reflexes with short spear thrusts. I countered each in turn and then spun in low under his attack, my war axe whirling. I flicked my wrist and scored two quick strikes just above the beast-man's knees, but the beast countered by striking my shoulder with the flat of his spear, instantly numbing it and causing me to drop my weapon. I rolled out of the way and pulled my bone dagger. It was not a weapon for war so much as a skinning tool, but my axe was gleaming at the beast-man's feet and I had no way to retrieve it safely.

Somewhere in the dark I heard another gurgling scream and then another. I have no doubt that while the men of my tribe were more than able to take on any man this side of the mountains; we were being soundly beaten by these massive brooding creatures. But I also heard the twang of Mok's bow as it struck home again and again, and that at least gave me a little hope that all was not lost.

The beast-man in front of me gave no pause to consider my dagger. Instead, he rushed in with a mighty thrust of his spear that I sidestepped easily enough, but too late I realized it was all a feint; the beast had foreseen I would spin out and away from him and had already begun a side swing with his spear that caught me in the chest before I had a chance to plant my feet.

I had underestimated their skill in battle and paid the price with a crushing blow that sent me reeling to the ground. In that moment the beast-man was upon me, smashing me with heavy fists like stones about the face and chest, and before I lost my breath and went to sleep I had a chance to see two of them descending on Mok, one riddled with arrows and still at fighting strength.

My enemy smashed my head into darkness.

I came around to the sound of my own heart beating strangely in my chest. When I opened my eyes I saw it wasn't my heart beating at all—it was the alien sound of the beast-man's drums that we had heard from the ridge of the valley. I tried to sit up discovered I was bound fast to a log by my hands and feet.

I was lying in the grass a short ways from the center of the camp. There were piles of meat around me; I recognized a half dozen separate deer carcasses, along with several other woodland creatures; rabbits, wolves, and even two bears. All had been killed in a similar fashion— they'd had their heads crushed by large stones and their bodies pierced by the terrible spears the beast-men carried. There was to be some sort of feast, I surmised; there was a heavy communal bonfire in the center of the camp that was easily three-men tall. It was rimmed with animal carcasses that the beast-men fed at will. A bit further out they danced and sang atonal melodies and beat their chests and stomped their feet in some sick perversion of song.

Across the fire from me I saw a huge chair, where sat the largest of the beast-men dressed in all the trappings of a chief. He wore a crown made of human jawbones stitched together with hair and strips of leather. I had no doubt what kind of leather that was, and it made me shudder down into the very depths of my being. The chief wore a cloak upon which was painted many red eyes and hungry mouths—what I could only surmise was in honour of some dark god that the beast-men worshipped—a nameless horror consisting of blind eyes and chewing mouths.

As I watched, two of the beast-men reached into the fire, pulled out the roasting body of one of my tribesmen, and neatly tore him in half. His organs spilled out through the tear with much slopping and sizzling on the hot stones around the fire; it would appear the beast-men had little use for properly cleaning their food before devouring it. Just as with the buck in the darkness of the forest, the men tore into the flesh of my kin like animals, rending the tastiest parts from bone and stopping only to offer up the head and heart to their chief, which gratefully he took. He devoured the heart in just a few bites, and then used his side teeth to crack open the skull and slurp the brains. The sound of it sickened me, and I had to bury my head in my shoulder to keep from crying out.

"Hey," a familiar voice said. "Are you awake?" It was Mok. I twisted my head toward the sound of his voice and saw he was bound in similar fashion to me on a separate log. His face looked much the same as mine felt—it was bloodied and black on one side from the bruising blows of the beast-man's fists.

"I am," I croaked.

"Did you see that?" he said, and I told him that I had.

"We are next," Mok said with certainty. "We are in the food pile for their feast."

"What can we do?" I said. "I am held fast by my bonds. I can barely move my head."

"It's leather. I think I know a way to get free."

I asked what it was, and he scowled for a moment before speaking. "I'm not sure it will work, but leather gets slippery when you wet it. And heat makes it stretch. So if we can use something warm and wet . . ."

". . . we may be able to get free," I said, and saw he was on to something. But what to use? I had nothing on hand. If I could reach my hands to spit on them or get water on them it might be easy, but they were bound tight around a log and I was unable to move them much. When I did, the bark on the log dug painfully into my flesh.

"Mok," I said. "Pull the binds. You may be able to gash your flesh enough to make the leather slippery.

"You speak the truth," Mok said, and then did something unexpected. He smiled and nodded at me. For the moment our petty war was over and we were equals.

There was no time to bask in the compliment, so I simply nodded. Then I leaned as far back as my position would allow and flexed my arms, driving my hands into the bark of the log. It was painful. In truth, it was agony; I ground the flesh of my hands against the bark as hard as I could and the pain of it nearly blinded me. I felt the skin reddening then tearing open, and then my fingers were sticky with fresh, hot blood.

The leather straps didn't loosen, but my heart gave thanks when my hands began to slide a little. It gave me hope and I tore them further, until I felt the bark scraping the bone of my broken hand and each scrape shot pain up my arms.

So intent on my task was I that I failed to see the approaching beast-men until they set hands on Mok. He screamed at them immediately, throwing every curse known to our people down upon them. They took no notice. I believe they had no sense of the human tongue, for the words Mok spoke would have enraged any man with sense, and the beast-men merely growled back and forth to one another. One reached down and grabbed Mok by the arm, and with a powerful yank they pulled it free of his log. Mok screamed and screamed; the bones in his arm snapped like twigs and I saw a spray of blood when the bones near his wrist crumpled and tore through his flesh.

The other beast-man pulled his leg free in a similar fashion, and I saw with horror the leather hadn't been broken down there. Instead, Mok's foot came clean off and now dangled by the strap attached to his other foot. It was also smashed badly, a misshapen and bloodied lump on the end of his leg. They lifted Mok up onto their shoulders the way two men might carry a stuck pig, and he screamed and screamed. I know what happened next but I didn't see it because I clenched my eyes to shut out the horror. Needless to say I couldn't also close my ears and I heard the roar of the beast-men as new meat was added to their feast. Mok's screams turned into screams as he was tossed into the cooking pit among the other meats.

His shrieks were short lived.

I pulled harder than I thought possible, my mind crazy with panic at the thought of being the next course in their feast. I pulled and rubbed until my hands went numb around the leather straps, and then suddenly, between the drumbeats, I heard the wing bone snap as my thumbs collapsed into my hand. Pain flashed in both arms like lightning bolts, and I slipped my palms through the leather straps. Barely conscious, I had little time to dwell on the mangled mess that was my hands. Instead, I pulled myself into a squatting position so I could reach around the log and grasp my ankles. It was difficult to untie the binds with slippery fingers and smashed thumbs, but at last I worked the knots free and got to my feet.

I was very careful about standing; I couldn't know how good the eyes of the beast-men might be and I was in no shape to fight even one of them. Instead I slipped over the log and skulked away from the feast and the fire into the cold black of night.

It was sometime later, after I had made it back up to the top of the valley, when I heard the sound of the drums stop. My escape had been discovered, because I swear by the gods I could hear the screams of their rage all the way at the top of the hills though their camp was far below. I didn't stop. There was no telling how far or how fast they could travel before the sun rose.

On the way home I passed our hunting camp and saw that wolves had been at our meat. I was careful not to touch any of it in case the beast-men were tracking by scent. Let them have their fill.

I walked on, taking time only to bind my hands. At last I made it home to the camp, and the rest you know. After my wounds were tended I was brought before the chiefs and made to recount my tale. And then, while they deliberated on a course of action, I was taken to my bed where sleep took me.

My words and wounds were enough to convince the tribal elders it was time to move on, to follow the herds to the north. They didn't say as much, but it was believed my story was the cause of the move, and I was grateful.

My dreams, since that night, have been haunted by the images of the giant beast-men in the bloody hills. I still see the look on poor Mok's face when they ripped him from that log like a piece of meat, and I awaken with the sound of those awful drums pounding in my ears. That night has become a living terror in my heart, from which I will never escape. I know this, because this evening, sitting by the fire, I hear those drums again, stretching out from the deepest parts of the hills and down onto the plains where we are now.

When I look toward the great black of the mountains I see the fevered orange light of their mighty fires and know that the beast-men of the Great Valley are still out there.

Tonight the fires are closer than ever, and the drums louder than they have been since that night, and I fear I may not live to see the morning. For days, we have had a rash of animals wandering through our camps as the totems of our gods; the deer and bear, wolf and rabbit and fox have all come down from the hills away from the fires and the drums. Our chiefs have decreed a blessing for our bounty, and all are singing the praises of the gods even as we strike these animals down and prepare for a huge feast in celebration.

Only I remain in the shadows, gnashing my teeth and spitting my warnings to all who will listen. The animals are here not as a blessing but as a warning, I cry, though none listen. Our gods are fleeing their homes and we are merely standing in the way.

The animals come because now there is something worse than men in the mountains, and they are coming this way.

A MOTHER'S SON

BY

D.G. SUTTER

DAY 1

THE AD IN the *Post* was meant to recruit young professionals eager to journey into the unknown. "Manifest Destiny," so they said, "to breach the Western Coast." Meriwether Lewis and William Clark had accomplished said feat years before, with the help of tracker Sakakawea or Sacagawea, but there was truly left much to discover.

It was a world open for pioneers, men of hard will. Wayland knew he possessed the determination to become great. He'd just never been granted the opportunity. After meeting with the commander of the future expedition—a straw chewing son-of-a-gun named Jeremiah—he knew it was time to pony up and excel. His mother had kissed him goodbye and waved him off before he trotted down the road to meet with Commander Jeremiah and his trapping brigade. They'd been hired out to transverse the territory west of the Black Hills, crossing over the same trail Lewis and Clark had endeavored upon nearly twenty years before. Wayland Marshall wasn't the youngest greenhorn at twenty-four, but he figured to be one of the least experienced. What he knew of survival was handed down from his father: only the simplest things, like how to spark a flint off of steel or load a rifle.

He knew not the tradition of fur trapping, which most of the brigade did, the "Mountain Men." When he rode upon the pack of men waiting on horseback, he saw they were hardened from years in the wild skinning hides and gnawing upon buffalo jerky.

They stared back at his nearly-beardless face covered in sparse stubble with no welcome, no console. In their eyes, he was just another disposable boy for the job. No introductions were made at first; they merely rode on in silence until out of town. Once clear of the town's borders, the trapping brigade picked up speed and Wayland was forced to follow suit, or be left in the uncharted. He started to wonder if he had made the right decision.

Day 4

For the first leg of the trip, traveling along the White River had been a pleasant steady trek. The view of the Great Plains was magnificent, and thriving off of buffalo stew and venison was right up Wayland's alley.

He had bonded with another of the younger Mangeur de Lards—or rookie trappers—with just a tad bit more experience. He had weathered two winters trapping and taught Wayland to spring a beaver trap and how to stretch the plew—beaver skin—over a small willow branch. They talked and joked, and threw their hunting knives into trees.

For the day they had small success on a tributary of the White, bringing in only twenty plews. Wayland's feet felt numb from standing in the cold October water. It was a beautiful thing when Jeremiah lit a bonfire of ash logs and he could warm his feet, though. He took his leather shoes off and reclined next to his new friend, Ben Naismith.

"Have you always desired to be an adventurer?" Ben asked while sitting on a stone.

"No, I wanted to be a shipper's apprentice, when I was a boy," Wayland said.

"What changed your mind?" Ben ripped a piece of buffalo jerky off and handed it to him.

He chewed on the tough, salty meat. It felt good in his restless stomach. "My father. He tried to raise me as a gamester. I never much liked the idea of killing another living being, and never really listened to him. When he died I figured it was the most I could do to support my mom and his honor."

Ben scratched one of his long sideburns. He grabbed his slab of dried meat and tore it with his incisors. Through a mouthful of carcass he said, "That's sure real nice of you."

"I guess," Wayland said under his breath. He missed his mother more than he thought he was going to, and hoped she was getting along fine.

"Now don't be modest," Ben said, shaking his strand of jerky at Wayland. "Takes a real man to look after his mother. You put that humble pie right back where you found it, Way."

Wayland scrunched his eyebrows. Nobody had ever called him "Way" before. Not to say he didn't like it. It showed that somebody on the expedition had an affinity for him. Even if he felt alone, Ben was there. He regretted that his mother didn't have a familiar reassurance.

Day 11

They finally found a spot to set up camp at the foot of the Black Hills. Jeremiah told them to expect a lengthened stay, for the beaver pelts were plentiful. He and Ben pitched a lean-to of willow branches, draped with leaves and branches to block the autumn wind.

Afterwards, Jeremiah had rallied Wayland, Harold—a big ole' man, six-foot-four and meat—and a man they called Smith. Ben would stay with the ten other Brigadiers in the streams, springing traps and trying to catch some fish. The troupe of four set out on foot to hunt some grass grazers.

Wayland's pack was heavy. It was full of medicine—a mixture of castor, nutmeg, cloves, and cinnamon—to bait the beavers, and other odd items he knew he should have left at camp. His bullet block hung from his shooting bag, slapping off his thigh. The older trappers poked fun at him for using a flintlock, but he thought it was the only way to hunt.

Smith and Harold waded away from Jeremiah and Wayland, past an outcrop of raspberry bushes on the left. They disappeared into the thicket of browning fruit bearers as Wayland and the commander lightly treaded through fallen leaves.

"Got to be real careful," Jeremiah said. "Buffalo'll charge ya'"

Along their left the plains stretched away toward the horizon, a flat expanse of blowing grass. On the right was the forest from which they had ventured. Wayland hadn't hunted buffalo before, just small prairie dogs and squirrel, and the idea of killing such a majestic creature made him sick to his stomach. However, he knew that army colonels and rich Europeans couldn't survive without their fur coated hats.

"Then what do you do?" Wayland asked.

"Shoot 'em between the eyes."

In order to shoot one needed bullets, and with the newly-implanted danger of a charging buffalo, Wayland found himself checking his shooting bag and bullet block to be sure he was well equipped with fifty-caliber. They walked quietly for some time before there was a sound of crunching ahead in the trees. Jeremiah held up his hand to stop Wayland. The greenhorn halted, pulled a bullet free of his block, and loaded the barrel of his rifle.

"Watch my back," Jeremiah said. "Don't fire unless you get a good shot. May be a deer."

As Jeremiah waded into the thicket, Wayland tried to steady his rifle to Jeremiah's left. It was shaking, but he kept his finger free of the trigger to guard against accidental fire. In front of the commander was a short hill, sloping to the right. It was shielded by a wall of pines, blocking Wayland's view of his commander.

Wayland crept closer, quietly stepping around leaves and twigs. He was almost around the trees—could even see Jeremiah's brown-clothed body cautiously working its way up the hill—when he stepped on a twig and it snapped.

He paused. He saw Jeremiah's body through the parts in the branches halt immediately. There was a rustling of branches snapping against each other . . . and snarling. Wayland stood stock still. A little ways away, Jeremiah raised his Hawken's rifle to eye level. His ears filled with an explosion, followed by a distant ringing. Gray gunpowder tempted the outskirts of his eyelids.

"C'mon," Jeremiah said.

Wayland tramped around the edges of the trees and saw laying there a gigantic brown animal, flat on its stomach. "What is it?"

"Grizzly. It was standing on its hind legs, reaching up for those apples," said Jeremiah.

After being shot the animal must have fallen forward, for Wayland could not see its head, just a mess of thick, deep brown fur. On top of the fell being was a patch of matted bloody fur. He swallowed hard. The sight was rather disheartening for the greenhorn.

"You sure it's dead?"

Jeremiah crouched fearlessly near the head. He closely examined the animal's back and, apparently considering it dead, lifted the skull off the ground. His eyes flashed wide and he stumbled backwards, landing on his bottom. The head thudded on the hard ground.

"I can't believe it!" he said.

Wayland clutched his rifle tightly in his hands. "What? What's wrong?"

"It isn't a grizzly. It looks like I've killed a man!" The commander placed an open hand over his mouth and exhaled like the north wind.

"That cannot be a man," Wayland said. "It's too hairy. Let's flip it."

He grabbed below the thing's waist and with all his might pulled up on the suit of hair. The man-beast flopped over reluctantly. Wayland looked upon the exit wound. Intestines spilled from the eight-inch hole. He brought his gaze to the face of the creature and was stunned at the apelike resemblance. It was on the verge of eight feet tall, with massive hands and feet, opposable thumbs included. The head was rounded and smoothed to a point at the peak. Lining the cheekbones was a thick mane, like a full beard. Green, glassy eyes stared toward the canopy above, seeming not to be focused on anything in particular.

Jeremiah stood and hovered over the body. "Thank God it's dead. Might as well bring it back to camp. No sense in wasting whatever it is."

He pulled from the contents of his shoulder pouch a long whistle and blew into it. "Harry and Smith'll find us. We'll be eating good tonight from this big lump."

The commander kicked the animal and the unmoving body absorbed the blow. Wayland's stomach turned over looking at the beast's bloody remains.

◆　◆　◆

When they returned to camp, Smith went about carving the animal like a butcher. He slit it from neck to waist and around the back, pulling the skin off in a rectangular sheet. Stomach still turning, Wayland couldn't watch any longer. He descended upon the stream where camp was set up. The fire had gone out; the only remains a pile of charred wood and black ash.

On the bank of the wide stream was a boat constructed of branches, with pelts pulled taut over the bottom and sides. It was flipped upside-down to dry out. Wayland knew it to be a bull boat. They were built to transport the beaver plews to the trading posts once the brigade had collected enough. Wayland figured Ben and the party must have built it and then worked further downstream—collecting bounties to fill the vessel—because they were nowhere in sight.

Wayland started to gather a pile of sticks into a teepee, to start a fresh fire. Underneath the stick monument, he placed dried grass and leaves for kindling. After mashing the flint on the small piece of steel, sparks floated into the small mound and the beginnings of the fire took. He blew upon the catalysts until the short logs were ablaze with the foreshadowing of a hot dinner. What type of meat they would be eating was another thought entirely, but Wayland was hungry enough that it no longer mattered. He was about ready to chew his own arm off.

It was a good fifteen minutes and adding of more fuel to the fire before Jeremiah was sauntering toward the stream where Wayland was checking the spring traps and baiting more medicine into them. Harold and Smith were on his heels, the latter carrying a two-foot long, rusted metal box. The commander held a pan filled with squared hunks of meat, which Wayland assumed to be of the hunted body. He could see, strung up to a tree, the remainder of the carcass—a large skeleton dripping blood with sporadic clumps of fur clinging to the bones.

Harold sat his large rump on one of the rocks with his back to Wayland and started to pick at his toenails. Wayland was taken aback when Smith aimed right for him, looking down into the box he carried.

"Hey, boy," Smith said.

Wayland stepped out of the stream, away from the nearby beaver dam. "Yes?"

Wayland hadn't liked the way Smith called him *boy*, but his father had taught him to respect his elders, even if they disrespected you.

"Take a look." Smith spun the box in his dirty hands. Inside was the head of the beast. It was on its side, staring at the wall of the box. "I'm gonna' hang it on my wall as a trophy."

"That's disgusting."

Wayland moved his tongue around in his mouth as if he'd tasted something profoundly awful. Smith cackled a tobacco-laced hack. His teeth were rotting in his mouth. He turned his curly head around to look upon his friends. "Boy doesn't like the idea!" He cackled loudly again and patted Wayland on the shoulder. "You'll be a man someday."

The experienced trapper turned, shaking his head. He sat down, also with his back to Wayland, and started to jabber with Harold. Anger wasn't a common emotion for Wayland, but he couldn't shake the desire to toss a rock at the back of Smith's head.

◆　◆　◆

The smell of pine needles was stronger than usual as Wayland tried to drift off to sleep on the mattress made from them. Ben and the brigade had returned not long after Wayland had eaten and gone to bed. He watched as they flipped the bull boat and filled it to the brim with pelts. His friend remained near the fire, drinking cheap whiskey and kidding around. Wayland couldn't stomach their utter disrespect for life.

Smith had said they were *just* animals. He simply couldn't stop thinking of the beast and how manlike it was. He tried to imagine animals not having feelings, not feeling pain, and it wasn't possible. He'd heard dogs whine and kittens purr.

Through the branches draped over the lean-to Wayland saw Ben and hoped he didn't share the same sentiments as the elders. He knew it was hypocritical to eat the creature and then be angry with the slaughterer. He just wished there was a better way.

He drifted in and out of sleep. At one point he became aware of Ben crawling into the lean-to and lying down on the pine needle mattress. The pungency of whiskey greeted his nostrils. It became colder throughout the night and Wayland knew the fire must have gone out. He scrounged with his feet for the bottom of the blanket, to stretch it over his entire body.

A thud awoke the dreaming greenhorn and he opened his eyes. After they adjusted to the drought of light Ben's body came into focus not more than two feet away. Wayland gasped at the proximity. He could still smell the whiskey on his friend's stale breath.

There was another thud and a far-off crunching of branches. Wayland propped himself onto his elbow. He tried to peer through the spaces in the shelter, but it was pitch black in the forest. He told himself if it was an animal, to go back to bed and it would go away, but when he laid his head down his brain didn't agree. He was too scared to sleep and too scared to stay awake. He thought of waking Ben, but didn't want to seem a scaredy-cat.

Grunts and heavy breathing came from the trees, and what sounded like leaves crunching under heavy feet. The sounds seemed so close that Wayland didn't dare move and attract attention. Instead, he focused on keeping his eyes open, ears listening, and his muscles ready for decisive action.

Slowly but surely the texture of the world started to really focus as his eyes fully adjusted to the dark. He could pick out the difference in size between the pine needles, and also the cracked lips of Ben, wide open and emitting short snores. Wayland wanted to plug his mouth. He was going to get them killed.

Somebody else must have heard the noises because there was a loud click and then an oil lantern flicked on. Wayland saw Smith's rough face covered in a gritty brown beard, peering into the darkness. He sat near the fire pit and leaned over to pick up his rifle. Struggling to his feet, his foot kicked the empty bottle of whiskey into the fire pit and then he tripped. The bottle smashed and Smith muttered, "Damn," under his breath.

The trapper stopped in the orange-yellow glow, his glossy eyes of inebriation staring higher than his head. He started to raise his rifle slowly, but before he could, simply yelled and tried to turn. A monstrous animal fell upon him, one nine feet high, with arms like a sideshow freak.

Wayland knew it must be one of the apes-creatures. It moved with grace despite its size, lifting Smith high in the air. Smith lunged at it with a closed fist, but it grabbed his arm with apparent calculation and sent a sickening snap into the night air. Smith screamed for help, but it was cut off when the monster grabbed both sides of his head and pulled it clean off like the top of a bottle. Blood bubbled out of the neck like a shaken beer, suddenly uncapped.

His body stood still for a moment and then fell forward onto the oil lantern. The lantern smashed into pieces and lit the headless corpse on fire. The beast took the head and bashed it on the sitting rock until it was only a handful of mush. It turned around and licked its giant paws clean.

It stood there flaring its nostrils and surveying the camp. The arms of the creature naturally hung further than its knees and when it walked they swung dramatically forward and back. For a second Wayland caught it looking at his lean-to, but it turned in the other direction.

He shook Ben. "Hey, wake up. Be quiet, but wake up!"

"Huh?" his drunken friend asked.

"There's an animal here . . . it killed Smith." Wayland hadn't realized before, but he was shaking. His fists were clenched in fear, so he released the tension.

"Killed him?" Ben asked as he began to sit up.

Wayland grabbed Ben's shoulder and pushed him into the pine needles. The sound of the short action made the beast turn face toward their shelter. Smith's body had completely lit on fire and the smell was awful, nothing but burnt hair and toasted flesh. The ape passed it by without a glance, working toward Wayland and Ben.

A shot rang out and the animal screamed a hearty roar as a piece of its shoulder flew off. It picked up speed then hunkered down quickly toward the lean-to. Wayland sat up and readied his knife. The thing leapt into the air and Wayland saw its bloodthirsty eyes in the light of the fire. It was driving off of feral instinct, fight instead of flight.

Ben was sobering up and was crouched near Wayland, trying to kick farther away from the falling beast. The only way out, however, was in the direction of the incoming hairy bullet. As it fell on the shelter, snapping the sides and falling forward, it raked a giant arm across the diameter of their fort.

Claws dug into Wayland's cheek and his head knocked into Ben's shoulder. Wayland gouged with his knife and felt it slice into something soft. He hoped it was the animal. Ben yelled and pushed off of him, trying to break through the side of the shelter that was still intact.

"Help! Get us out of here!" Ben yelled in an unexpectedly high-pitched voice.

Wayland had a second to breathe after noticing the beast's neck was sliced wide open. The attacker hung limply across the broken branches of the lean-to, the supports puncturing the animal's broad chest and poking out the back. He wanted no responsibility for its death and hoped it died painlessly, before he slit its throat.

"Let's get out of here," Ben said. "I'm too cramped up. I need some fresh air."

Wayland climbed through the hole which had been created by the giant animal's onslaught. He made sure not to touch it, for fear of it coming back to life. Ben—still apparently tipsy—staggered through the opening behind Wayland.

"What in the hell? We're lucky to be alive, man." Ben bent over, placing his hands above his knees. He let out a puff of air and stood up, stretching his short arms over his head. It was an odd time to compare, but Wayland considered Ben to be half the size of the dead ape lying in their sleeping quarters.

Ben's eyes drifted over the forest as Jeremiah, rifle in hand, stumbled near to the fire.

"You boys okay?" He was still in his under trousers. His usually long jovial face looked drawn in the wan light.

"No, no . . ." Ben said, pointing at the trees. His eyes reflected the firelight of the burning corpse. "Hundreds of eyes . . . hundreds in the branches."

Wayland looked to the canopy of the forest. The trees were filled with glowing green eyes, briskly moving toward the camp in bumpy movements. Jeremiah raised his rifle to the canopy and started to fire. Gunpowder obscured Wayland's vision, but he could hear the arrival of other trappers, asking what was happening and loading their rifles.

"Fire into the trees, we're under attack," Jeremiah said. He packed a bullet into the barrel of his gun and raised it into the sky.

Wayland ran to retrieve his rifle and cleared the smoke. His ears were ringing, but he heard the roars of the approaching beasts. It sounded like a war cry. Before he could reach the destroyed lean-to the apes had descended from the branches.

He came to a brisk stop. There were three of them surrounding the fort. The beast on the left was a grayish color; it barreled for Wayland on all fours. The greenhorn put up no fight. He turned and sprinted full speed through the chaos and toward the brigade. Bullets whizzed past his body. None of them hit, but with the amount of adrenaline coursing through his body the pain would have most likely been numbed completely.

The trappers shot at the trio of animals. Wayland didn't turn to look. There were too many creatures to try and fight. One of them landed on top of Jeremiah's shoulders, ripping his chest down the middle with extended claws. It pounded on his back with closed fists, hammering Jeremiah into the earth.

Wayland didn't slow, but instead changed his direction. He headed for the bull boat and dove into the floating device. Using his knife he sawed at the rope that connected the boat to shore.

"Ben!" he yelled into the fight.

The creatures didn't seem concerned with the man in the boat; they were creating carnage amongst the trappers on land. He couldn't see Ben and resigned to lie down in the pelts, in the hopes of being overlooked. Rifles continued to go off for a short period and Wayland heard Harold crying for it stop. Eventually his pleas were cut off with a gargled scream.

There was movement outside of the boat, the subtle lapping of water against the sides along with inhuman groans. Wayland heard footsteps in the sand and his heart quickened. The boat rocked as something landed next to him. He felt the thing near his face, so he turned to look. Ben's eyes reflecting the fire stared deadly back at him.

He tried to stay calm, but started to hyperventilate. More feet crunched in the sand and kicked grains into the water, causing tiny splashes. He didn't want to know how many of them were out there. He closed his eyes.

Heavy objects started to rain into the boat, hitting him all over his body—round and hair covered objects. Wayland cried, not only for himself, but the trapping brigade. Where he had once felt sorrow for the dead animals, he no longer did. At the start he had figured them for nothing more than wild creatures resolved to killer instinct, but these creatures—they understood. They had come not for food or to protect their territory, but for vengeance.

Warm liquid seeped into his sleepwear, drenching his arms and legs, the sides of his body. He thought of his father and mother. She would miss him. Then, he thought, would his father be proud?

"For your honor, Father," he said with a sigh.

Gripping his deer knife, he flipped the boat over. The trappers' heads bobbed in the water like fishing tackle in the space beneath the boat. The pocket of air would be enough to keep him alive for a long time.

The bottom of the boat came crashing down on his head, a loud *thump* echoing inside his skull. He bit his tongue. Blood leaked out between his lips. A pair of hairy hands wrapped around his legs. Wayland bent forward in the water and stabbed with the knife at the appendages. They retracted. Another pair of hairy hands wrapped over his arm, tugging him underneath the surface. He stabbed through the hand, but when the creature pulled away the knife went with it.

His shoulder was grasped by an exceedingly strong claw and he was yanked to the floor of the stream. He kicked beneath the water with all of his might. A pair of wet, hairy hands wrapped over his head . . . and began to squeeze.

Day 8

Dear Mother,

I know that most likely I shall never send this letter, for the post does not travel this route, but I figured on the small chance they should pass I would write you. The wilderness is more than I have ever imagined. One hears stories, but can never truly grasp the awe in witnessing firsthand the beauty of the plains.

Of late I have been sick for home. I was never meant for hard labor. I was raised under your hand, not Father's, and felt I needed to do right and attempt his work. He so wanted me to be his son. I feel alone without you here and cannot wait to see your rosy face, greeting me on our doorstep. I have met a friend, and that is indeed a glorious thing! However, the work is tireless and the days drag on and on. I long for a cup of your homegrown tea and a good book.

The others jest at my reluctance to kill, so you might think of me a weak man, but as I have said, I am not cut-out for this labor. I have been gone a mere week and already my feet ache something fierce, and my back is out of sorts. I realize after much introspection that I might not be as manly as the other trappers, but I have realized what makes me more human. I so dearly wish I would have heeded your advice, and never have gone on this dreaded expedition. I shall write you sooner than later.

Sincerely and always,

Wayland

MEAL TICKET

BY

KEVIN MILLIKIN

WITH A QUICK and mighty shove, the hairy beast threw the tree to the ground. The tree screamed out with a thunderous crack, reminiscent of nails dryly ripped from a board. The Sasquatch howled at the sound. Spittle and foam seethed from his dark lips as he clinched his massive palm against the bloody gash that ran through his upper arm and out the back in a serrated, gore-laden star that clotted itself with matted fur and severed flesh.

The Sasquatch ran headlong into the dense woods that comprised the Colville National forest that made up the Northeastern edge of Washington State. He only knew of it as home and these men, these ungodly creatures, had encroached upon his sanctuary with a sense of violence uncalled for in this wild place.

They were still behind him. The Sasquatch heard them perfectly as he dodged to and fro throughout the trees and leapt over the rocks. They were somewhere in the darkness laughing, yelling and calling for him in the diminishing distance. Their voices masked beneath his monstrous footfalls.

One of them laughed. "Where'd ya go?"

"Come on back 'ere an' make us rich, you freak!"

The third one in the pack was silent, and it was that one that scared the beast the most. The others were loud and obnoxious, distinguishable by their *human* scent of bad hygiene and beer, while the other was a cougar, lying in wait. A predator fit for the fight.

Trees and brush blurred together in the deepening twilight. The beast had traversed these lands thousands of times in the many seasons since his birth, but now the woods that comprised his dwelling engulfed him, filling him with a constricting sense of fear he never thought imaginable as he found himself driven further into the tress by the hunters that quickly closed the gap between him and his survival.

The Sasquatch stopped in a clearing; his breathing was labored, second only to the rattling breath that he failed to catch. He balanced himself from foot to foot; dead grass and twigs crunched and snapped beneath his massive feet as the surrounding world slowly morphed into a blur. The pain in his arm had grown immense and blinding, leaving him in a state of near suffocation, but he knew he needed to survive for *her*; it was that will alone that pushed him forward toward a lone outcropping of boulders just beyond the clearing.

In a moment of complete and utter hopelessness, the Sasquatch pressed his body against the boulder's smooth stone surface, contemplating his next move. The resulting sensation was relaxing, reviving. As his sweat-drenched fur met the cold stone it gave him a sharp jolt that snapped him from his fears and released him from the pain.

The Sasquatch took his enormous hand off the wound; it stung in the gentle breeze, but he found this pain had been a good thing. It reminded him he was alive. As he held his enlarged palm out in front of his face he watched as his blood turned black beneath the vanishing sun as it weaved and slid through the tangled web of fur. He furiously grunted at the gory sight. The Sasquatch's fear quickly turned to hatred as he heard the men approach with the crunching of careless footfalls through the leaves.

◆ ◆ ◆

They had been in the woods now for the better part of a week with little to no results and not even a single kill to either of their names. The white-tailed deer that where typically plentiful around these parts might have been a mere myth this time around.

Earl, Rocky and Spencer had spent most of their day trampling through and lying in the brush, whispering dirty jokes and drinking from their surplus of beer when they finally decided to call it a day.

"Hold up," Spencer said, bringing the other two men to a sudden halt.

"What's up?" Earl asked as his instincts switched from Earl Mann the mechanic into Earl Mann the survivalist.

They stood in silence, ears poised against any foreign sound. It started with the rustling of leaves and the swaying of branches that eventually evolved into the occasional hoot of an owl and the scamper of small rodents.

"What you listening to?" Rocky said.

Rocky had complained the whole day about being hungry, and if he did it again, Earl knew he was going to hit him. He glared at his lesser counterpart and listened patiently in an act of defiance against his partner's wishes. He heard it, too. It was a low growl that came across the forest, carried with the Northern breeze. A beastly sound matched with the rustle of fabric and the inevitable ripping of cloth to which they all froze, gasps held tightly in their lungs. The knowledge they weren't alone in the woods flooded them with a momentary rush of panic before the realization sunk like a stone into Earl's cranium.

"The camp!" he hissed, breaking from the pack to charge through the woods like a lone soldier storming the beach.

The other two men weren't far behind and the three-man army stampeded through the brush with their simple, yet-well-kept rifles shouldered and ready. Earl took the lead, paving the path. He was followed close in second by Spencer, with Rocky puffing away in the rear.

"Damn guys, it's probably nothing," Rocky wheezed.

"I don't want to hear it, soldier," Spencer said in a mock military tone.

"Yeah, yeah."

Every footstep pulled them closer to the camp. The ravenous sounds became more pronounced. Every crash and rip causing the three of them to quicken their pace until even Rocky was caught up in a full-blown run.

Earl's green, fair weathered pick-up truck Lucille came into view. Its windows had been smashed, discarded cigarette packs, gutted seat cushioning and fast food wrappers littered the ground like overindulgent viscera.

Earl skidded to a slow stop with Spencer and Rocky all but colliding into him like an old Three Stooges skit.

"No, no. Oh man, no," he cried. He fumbled with his rifle as if it was an extension of his manhood as tears began to well within his line of sight, blurring the dusk into a grey haze as his sorrow grew.

The camp remained unseen, hidden through a thicket of brush so as to not alert the resident Forest Rangers about their little combination of alcohol and firearms, and yet what seemed like a genius idea at the time now appeared to be little more than a curtain for a possible ambush. Still, with only a barrier of greenery between them and *it*, the threat of attack grew more plausible as the sounds slowly morphed into a low series of guttural grunts.

"Could it be a bear?" Rocky whispered. He stood close behind Earl, his low voice echoing loudly in his ear.

"Naw," Earl whispered in response. "Where'd they been hiding, then?"

"We ain't seen nothing but squirrels and 'coons since we've been here," Spencer added as if to drive the point home.

Earl cupped his free hand across his mouth and shouted, "Hey you!"

The persons unknown grunted back as if it was in response. Their movement ceased and together both parties listened anxiously to the silence of the other and in a matter of many slow-ticked seconds another grunt signaled the start of renewed movement.

"You hear that?" Rocky whispered. "Whatever it is, it's walking 'round there upright like a person would." His voice grew rigid with fright. "Ain't no animal that does that!"

"Bears move upright, you imbecile," Spencer said.

"Ah," Rocky groaned.

"We can hear you in there," Earl said. "And lemme tell you, you're messing with the wrong crew 'cause we *all* got guns." Earl rocked back on forth on the balls of his feet as he waited for a response that never came. "All right buddy," he yelled, cradling his rifle against his shoulder. "Okay, I warned ya'!" He fired a round above the trees.

The movement ceased once again and through deafened ears they heard a monstrous howl that pierced the evening sky, shaking them to the core.

And then the beast charged.

Trees and brush flew by the wayside with a nauseating *crunch* as the intruder burst from their cover.

"Man . . ." Earl muttered, but his words came almost as an afterthought because before he could even finish a humongous humanoid figure collided against him. The impact sent him—to the ground, air knocked from his lungs as his rifle slipped from his grip. Spencer and Rocky stumbled back as he fell at their feet.

From the ground, Earl watched with mounting horror at the beast of legends stood before his hunting party. The creature was humanoid with a thick blanket of fur that howled as it raised its arms to the heavens with a banshee's sneer, revealing rows of crooked, dagger like teeth that dribbled warm salvia down its jowls. Rot permeated from its open mouth, spraying the three good ol' boys with rancid spittle.

Earl's pulse raced in his ears.

Out of the three, Rocky was the one that acted first and in a singular moment of redemption, he stepped forward and pulled the trigger just as the beast lunged toward them.

The shot went wild. Poor aiming and quick, un-thought actions missed the mark, but still the Sasquatch staggered back. With a hellish shriek it grabbed violently at its arm. Droplets of blood sprinkled across the ground.

It took no time for the Sasquatch to regain its composure. A mix of emotions played out through its massive obsidian eyes, the type of emotion that transcends any species-*fear*-and with a parting howl the beast turned, running into the night.

Earl knew that his friends' act of bravery might have just damned them all.

◆　◆　◆

The Sasquatch seethed with unfathomable anger as the hunters continued onward in their approach. Their actions and every bit of their existence grew more exact and truthful in the wild man's ears and he knew—knew beyond the shadow of a doubt that it was kill or be killed and while the wound still stung, the beast primed himself for battle.

Beyond the boulder, a voice asked, "Where you think he went?"

Too which another replied, "Maybe he's bleeding out somewhere. I shot him pretty good. Who knows, maybe I killed him?"

"Please, I saw it and I saw that you shot him in the arm. Ain't nothing gonna die that way, but you scared him though, that's what you did."

The Sasquatch couldn't understand the language in which they spoke and rather then waste his precious moments trying to figure it out, he set about searching the ground for something, anything that he could use.

A small tree, only a few meters in length, lay dead in the leaves. Its once sturdy exterior was now a weakened carcass riddled with rot but still managed to retain a hint of its former strength. The Sasquatch touched the log before moving his massive paw across to a small stone that lay hidden and submerged beneath the dead foliage. He picked up the stone and bounced it across his furry knuckles, testing its weight. The rock was heavy, but not to the extent he needed. So, after shifting its weight into his wounded hand the beast crouched in the darkness and reached for the fallen tree.

A smile crossed his seasoned lips as he squeezed his mitts around the deadwood, brandishing it like a club. With his weapon in hand the beast agonizingly heaved the stone against one of the neighboring trees. The rock *clanked* off of its face, taking splintered chunks of bark with it as it fell.

◆　◆　◆

"Hold up," Spencer said as he sped up to take the lead. Spinning on his heels he turned to face the group. "What was that?"

Rocky shrugged. "I dunno."

Earl remained silent.

"Sounded like something fell," Spencer said.

"No," Earl said. "It sounded like something was thrown."

Spencer looked over his shoulder, back into the unknown. "You might be right."

Earl grumbled something in response. He *knew* he was right, but managed to bite off his words. "Let's just get a move on it," he finally said after a long pause. "I just wanna get this sucker bagged as soon as possible."

Spencer nodded and led the pack into the darkness. Earl couldn't complain. Usually he was the one in charge, but after seeing the damage the Sasquatch could do, he couldn't say boo about being second in tow.

"How much you think it'll be worth?" Rocky asked.

"I dunno," Spencer replied. "Good million or so, I reckon, just for its corpse."

"That's what I was hoping. What do you think he'd be worth if we snagged him alive?"

Earl spat, "I ain't taking the monkey unless it's dead." His words stunk of venom. "You saw it attack when we scared it back there. Just imagine what it'll be capable of when we get it backed into a corner."

After a couple moments of silence, Rocky replied, "You're right."

"I know."

◆　◆　◆

Sasquatch squatted against the massive boulder. Both hands clung tightly against the base of the log until the beast's enlarged knuckles bulged from beneath its leathery skin. He held onto his hate as he listened to the hunters' useless dialogue and found it took every ounce of will not to forget his plan and charge them headlong, but as their voices continued to grow nearer, mere feet away, even that decreased rapidly.

"What about jerky?" asked the runt in the back of the litter as they rounded the boulder. Sasquatch watched from the darkness as they passed unknowingly by him. Again, the small one asked: "What do you think Bigfoot would taste like if we turned 'im into jerky?"

Sasquatch howled as he leapt from the shadows. The men froze in a moment of shock as the beast's massive bulk charged at them, swinging the log around in a brilliant arc.

The old wood split as it impacted the lead hunter's face. Jagged bits of skull shot out, slicing through the beast's face as the broken tree wrapped itself around the bridge of the man's nose, erupting chunks of grey and crimson skyward in a marvelous geyser.

The hunter's final words, "No not yet . . ." gargled from his lips as he slumped to the ground.

The pudgy runt screamed as the other one readied his rifle, but before he could off fire a shot, Sasquatch threw the remaining husk of tree at him. The man ducked, firing his well-aimed shot into the ground, devastating his chance. Before he could recover, the Sasquatch ripped the weapon from his powerless hands and hurled it at the fat one when he turned to make a run for it. The rifle barrel whacked the runt upside the back of the head, sending the poor sod face first into the ground.

Sasquatch turned his attention back on the other man, but howled in rabid disbelief as the coward scrambled into the night, falling head over heels just for his chance to escape. The beast watched him for a moment longer until the man's frantic footfalls failed in entice him anymore.

Turning his focus back to the fallen runt, Sasquatch stepped toward the unconscious soul. His gigantic footfalls shook the earth with each thunderous step. The fallen hunter rolled onto his back. The man's chubby face was flushed red as blood trickled from a deep lesion that cut a jagged line across his brow. Dirt, twigs and leaves clung to the gore as his unfocused eyes quickly grew wide.

He screamed, "No, I'm sorry, no please don't! Please don't!" He shook his head in fevered protest as the Sasquatch drew nearer.

The beast growled, ribbons of drool leaking from his lips as he reached for the screaming child of a man. The Sasquatch wrapped his long fingers around the man's scalp as if he was merely palming something as simple as a ball.

The man continued to scream as the massive giant effortlessly plucked him up from the ground.

Sasquatch howled again, leveling the trembling man to meet his fiery gaze. The hunter looked back at his captor; his eyes were glossy slivers that peered out from beneath the beasts hairy knuckles.

His cries quickly turned to whimpers as his released his bowls down the leg of his pants. The rancid aroma stung the beast's eyes as he held him away like spoiled fruit.

"Please, don't," the man sobbed.

Sasquatch simply sneered as he threw the oaf against the boulder behind him. A yelp mustered forth from the man's lungs, plunging his world into darkness.

The beast watched as the man's body fell limp. Sasquatch eyed him, studied him, as his chest slowly rose and fell, reminding him of a sleeping bear cub. Sasquatch loudly exhaled–and with a grunt dragged the man to his feet before hurling him over his shoulder like a fleshy sack of potatoes. His face slapped across the beast's lower back; his arms dangled listlessly toward the ground.

Sasquatch howled, swinging the man against the boulder.

The man's pudgy face smashed with a moist *plop* as the Sasquatch cocked his arms back and swung again. Bones burst like clouds raining blood with every pronounced swing until all that remained of the hunter's face was a glistening bowl of pulp pooled within his skullcap.

Sasquatch grunted as he tossed the corpse aside and looked off into the darkness. As the beast sucked in deep lungful of air, his pulse raced as he grew more excited and he knew there was only one more. Just one more to kill until he and his kind would all be safe again.

◆　◆　◆

Earl had been pulling himself through the brush since spraining his ankle a half mile back. He cried out as his tough guy façade quickly faded as he began to cry.

Rocks, twigs and thorn bushes sliced his skin until he bled from dozens of scrapes and gashes that left his exposed flesh pock-marked by bloody ribbons.

Earl crawled until his lungs cried, burning for rest. His vision blurred, birthing a migraine that tickled its way across his scalp. He couldn't even force himself to stop and rest. No, not with Rocky's frenzied screams egging him on to move faster.

Earl forced himself back to his feet and gingerly stepped down on his twisted ankle. He yelped, yanking it back up as he wobbled on one foot. Bracing himself against a nearby tree he tried it again until he got bearable results and began his trek further into a part of the wilderness he had never before ventured.

"It's not fair," he grumbled as his deprived lungs burned for nourishment. "You were supposed to be my meal ticket." He didn't care that his friends were gone. Instead, he mourned the loss of the truck as well as the spoils of the hunt.

Somewhere nearby a twig snapped, the sound of which brought Earl to a sudden halt. He winced, breath catching in his throat as the pain in his ankle sung at him in an off-key harmony. But he sucked down his cries, not daring to alert the beast to his presence. He waited, listened, before he heard it again—the snapping of twigs and crunching of leaves.

Pivoting on his good foot, Earl spun around in near darkness and found he was unable to pinpoint the location

Panic and bile forced their way up his throat as a small rock cut through the darkness, coming to rest against his boot.

"No," he breathed as a howl rose through the night like the call of a wolf. "No!" He spun around, limping his way into a haphazard dash. His ankle shot bolts of lightning through his leg, the fire settling in his belly. He had no choice but to go with it, undeterred in his quest to survive.

Another howl and another rock found their way through the night, moving quick and hitting hard. The howl jolted him forward and he struggled for footing when the rock pelted him across his back, stinging him with the fury of a giant wasp.

Earl screamed, falling to the ground in a stunned heap of helpless flesh.—He stared upward, watching the stars that poked through the tree branches.

His mind slowed, he throat burned. Life itself lagged. His throat grew tight, the pressure lessened. It took him a moment to realize it wasn't his own reckless nerves that had brought him down but the thick, hairy arm that extended out from behind the trees, clothes–lining him where he stood. Earl struggled to grasp the situation as his eyes locked on the hairy branch.

How could he . . . ?

Was he truly running *from* Bigfoot and not *toward* him like an open invitation this whole time? Maybe he had gotten turned around somewhere and backtracked without realizing it.

Earl didn't know. All he knew was the Sasquatch that stepped from behind the tree was somehow different. He couldn't put his finger on it as his nerves were too frayed. This time, the beast looked smaller than before as well as a lighter shade of brown compared to the... other one. Earl whimpered and scooted further back across the ground.

"No . . ."

This new beast failed to move. Instead, it just stood there, looking at him with curious eyes.

The Sasquatch howled, but the howl did not come from the one that stood in front of him but the one that had caused him so much pain.

"You can't do this!" Earl screamed, voice raw. He spun around to face the other beast that stood on the path he'd just traveled.

Running wasn't an option. He was trapped. Hopelessly sandwiched between the two beasts, Earl's body trembled in the presence of death as the larger of the two stepped forward. It held its wounded arm tightly in front of it almost as though it intended for him to see it one final time as a reminder of *why* he had to die.

Earl's cries turned to screams as the Sasquatch stepped closer, looking down at him as if he was nothing less than a feeble insect. Earl flinched, feeling the monster's harsh criticisms staring him down through its black eyes. It was then the Sasquatch lifted its big foot off the ground.

"Not like this. You were my meal ticket," Earl whimpered through a bout of tears just before the Sasquatch stomped down on his face.

THE 100-YEAR BRAWL

BY

BOWIE V. IBARRA

1900
Near the Frio River
30 miles outside of San Uvalde

THE TWO MEN hiking the country trail heard the horn loud and clear as its sound danced across the dusty brush land near Concan, Texas. It was an ancient sound, the sacred clarion call the humanity deep in Ricardo's heart recognized with precision, forever carved in humanity's collective unconscious.

It was a call to arms, a call for battle.

"Was that it, Ricardo?" asked the man, shivering slightly from excitement. "Was that the . . . a horn for this so-called ritual?"

"That's got to be it, *Senor* Biediger," said Ricardo. "I'm not one hundred years old so I wouldn't know what it sounds like. *Comprendes?* But I'm sure that's it."

"Well, I didn't think I could trust *someone* like you," said Mr. Biediger with an air of impudent contempt. "But it looks like this will be a positive endeavor after all. Just don't drop the camera equipment."

The subtext from Biediger was clear, but Ricardo brushed it off. It wasn't the first time anyone had given him a backhanded compliment. He responded, "Oh, I won't. It belongs to my family, after all."

Ricardo carried a large case in both hands. He was short, but strong. He wore slacks with a white button-up shirt that was dusty from use. A plaid vest wrapped the shirt, and a red bandana hung around his neck.

"So, has anyone in your family seen this ritual?" asked the professor, hiking forward through the brush, the two of them follow the distinct sound of chatter and primitive music.

"Like I told you," said Ricardo, thinking, *Pinche viejo.* "My great-grandfather did."

"Well, apart from your great-grandfather."

"No," said Ricardo, shaking his head. "He passed down this story that was supposedly passed onto him. My grandpa told me the tale. So did my papa. It's March. It's 1900. Looks like we got lucky. Every hundred years, this great ritual of monsters happens by the old salt peder cave."

"A spring ritual, I would guess? That's what I initially thought when I first heard this story."

"More of a sacrifice is what it sounds like."

"Very common among primitive cultures. I assumed this ritual might fall on the spring equinox. These primitive cultures were aware of the changing of the seasons. I don't know how these so-called monsters could figure that out, however. Maybe they're smarter than we think?"

The sounds grew louder as they approached the location, which felt to Ricardo only yards away now. A set of trees seemed to hide what they were looking for in the distance. His heart beat with anticipation. He knew they were close.

They hiked in stunned silence until they cleared the tree line, reaching a cliff side overlooking a large, brushy clearing below. Gathering in that clearing were things they had never seen in their lives: large and hairy giants.

"Goodness," muttered Mr. Biediger, looking down in awe into the clearing below.

"*Dios mio*," whispered Ricardo, making the sign of the cross before he began to set up his camera.

They could not believe their eyes. The massive and hairy monsters were unbelievably large. Their bodies were covered with hair in most places and big muscles were noted rippling below the hair on their arms and legs. Their appendages were like tree trunks. Their shoulder muscles were so huge it made the monsters appear like they had no neck. Their eyes were wide. Their nose was more of a snout. White teeth contrasted against their dark brown skin. Their hands were huge, with long fingers. Their genitals hung low, swinging with their movements. They were bizarre throwbacks to mysterious beasts.

"Where do they come from?" asked Professor Biediger.

"Center of the earth, maybe," said Ricardo. "Or underground. *Yo no se.*"

"There are a lot of caves around this area, perhaps from there. They might sink deep into the earth. There's just so many. If they lived above ground, we would know it."

"Well, this is the battle they . . ."

Then Ricardo stopped, remembering something. "*Senor.* Biediger, wear this," he said, taking a necklace charm from his vest pocket. He put one on his own neck and offered the other to Biediger.

"What's this?"

"It's a charm, something that will protect us from the monsters. My great grandfather passed it down through the generations. He found it at the battle he saw. He said it protects us from them."

Biediger looked at the charm. It was nothing more than a bird feather and a bone tied together. It was strung to a leather necklace that hung around his neck.

"Nonsense, boy," said Biediger, smugly waving his hand. "With respect to your family, keep it for yourself."

Ricardo just shrugged and continued to set up the camera.

"This is amazing. Absolutely amazing," said Mr. Biediger, watching the activity with keen interest.

Below, several distinct groups of creatures were gathering. They had organized in crowds, seemingly indicating their loyalties and duties.

"Just like Grandpa said. The dark brown monsters fight the dark gray monsters," said Ricardo, indicating their fur.

"What do you mean, fight?"

"They fight. They have a certain game they play. We're about to see it."

"And you're not going to tell me any anymore? You're lucky your vague claim even got me out here."

"You're going to see it soon enough," said Ricardo, prepping the gunpowder for the flash. "It's a vicious game."

"It sounds like . . . like a primitive tribal ritual. A war ritual. Those must be the, well, the families." He pointed at a mass of what seemed to be females, older and slower-moving monsters, and very young beasts. The females were distinctly different than the children and the older ones. They had large, hairy breasts. The older monsters seemed slumped over. Some were missing appendages. "Curious," said the professor. "Have you noticed some of the monsters in that crowd outside of the revelers are missing arms?"

"*Verdad?*" said Ricardo, looking down. "You're right. And I think we're about to find out why."

"And over there. There are the musicians."

"Dad said monsters would be playing music. It's the music we've been hearing all this time," said Ricardo. "That's them."

A gray monster and a brown one held conch shells to their mouths, blowing their sacred sound. A group of nine or ten slapped heavy sticks together in rhythm, while another group clicked rocks together. Neither the rocks nor sticks were carved in any manner. They seemed to have been picked randomly for the sound they made. But it still created music, and the beasts chanted with that music.

"Where did they get conch shells?" asked the professor.

Ricardo just shrugged. "It looks to me those are clearly the warriors."

On both sides of the field, close to ninety yards apart, dozens and dozens of beasts were chanting and shouting in a frenzy of primal aggression. Ricardo continued setting up the camera as they both observed the ritual.

Another horn sounded, and both groups assembled in lines.

"This is looking more and more like sport," said the professor. "But why?"

"Who knows?"

"Maybe to crown a new leader?"

Ricardo noticed something. "The grays look like they're in trouble."

"Indeed," said the professor, seeming to have noticed the same. "Looks like the browns have a numbers advantage on the grays."

"And look how the smaller monsters are in the front rows and *los mas grandes* are in the back rows."

"You're right," said the professor. "Fascinating."

Music began from the monsters banging the drums, and a coordinated dance—a war dance—began from the brown faction, judging by how they chanted in a primal language, slapping their bodies and making threatening gestures at the grays.

"Snap a picture, man," said Biediger. "Snap a picture."

"Way ahead of you, *senor*," said Ricardo. A puff of smoke emanated from the gunpowder flash as he took the first picture. He immediately prepped another one as the brown group finished their dance. The monsters that supported the brown group cheered.

Then, the grays did a war dance of their own.

"Fascinating," said Professor Biediger yet again. He watched as the music died and the grays finished. Their spectators cheered with primal excitement.

Then, both sides assembled, holding very large stones in each hand.

"Here it comes," said Ricardo, prepping the camera.

"What?"

"The rain of stones."

"What?"

Ricardo readied another picture. "Watch."

The audience of beasts fell silent. The walls of monsters grunted, bounced, and steadied themselves for combat.

A drumbeat sounded.

Then a pause.

Another drumbeat.

Another pause.

The sound of a horn cut through the silence.

From the brown faction, the monsters lobbed a volley of large stones through the sky, arcing precisely toward the grays.

"Oh no . . ." whispered Mr. Biediger as Ricardo snapped a picture.

The stones arced gracefully through the sky, casting a shadow over the land briefly as they careened downward.

"They're just standing there," said Biediger, watching the grays hold their ground, growling and waiting to absorb the attack. "Why are they just standing there?"

"*Machismo*, I guess," said Ricardo.

With glorious and inhuman thuds, the rocks struck the grays. The rain of stones pummeled the beasts with horrifying cruelty. Though some monsters fell to the ground, having been struck directly in the head by the rocks, many still stood tall, frenzied, and furious. Ricardo and Professor Biediger watched in amazement. Some deflected rocks with their own stones. Others deflected the stones with their arms. Still others caught them.

"*Dios mio*," said Ricardo, cringing at the cracking of rocks across bodies and heads of the beasts.

"Do you realize how much strength it would take to heave a stone like that as far as they did?" asked the professor. "These things are powerful!"

"*Chingonones*. But I told you that already."

A lone beast broke from the group, running completely away from the battle and into the countryside as the remaining beasts stood tall. The beasts remaining cheered and growled in temporary triumph along with their supporters on the sidelines. If Ricardo and Professor Biediger could recognize war music, the sound of wild approval was just as recognizable.

Then, a burning silence fell on the crowd. The drums beat twice and the horn sounded. It was the gray's turn. They heaved their stones.

"Unbelievable," said Biediger. "Absolutely unbelievable."

Ricardo waited for the next volley to curve down out of the sky and strike the waiting brown army. As the stones found their mark, Ricardo snapped a picture.

The strategy of the browns was the same. They absorbed, deflected, dodged, or caught the heavy projectiles. Two of their ranks ran into the brush, away from the event. The remaining, still numbering more than the grays, reveled in triumph.

The drums beat rapidly as the two teams moved about twenty yards into the battlefield before setting up their lines again. Their ranks had diminished, leaving the bodies of their fallen comrades behind them. If the beast could still stand and had the courage to stand and fight in spite of the injuries, he moved forward.

Shortly, each team was ready for another round.

"Here it goes again," said Professor Biediger as the browns lobbed rocks at the grays. The same defensive strategy of absorbing, catching, or deflecting stones was employed, and more grays fell. The rocks diminished their numbers, but none ran away.

Cheers. Silence. Drums.

The grays attacked with their stones, reducing the browns by a few more. Two more ran off as the browns celebrated.

"Here it comes, *senor*," said Ricardo, prepping the camera for the next event. "*Chingasos, senor. Chingasos* like humans have never seen before."

One horn sounded. Then another. The two groups were snarling and chanting in their primal language as the third horn blew, unleashing the two savage hordes in a mad dash toward each other.

"My goodness," shouted Biediger as Ricardo snapped another picture of the monstrous hordes charging their lines, colliding with each other like mammoths.

Fists flew. Faces were scratched and torn away. Knees kneed bodies and legs. Eyes were gouged. Genitals attacked. Limbs were broken and torn away from their bodies. Monsters were tossed into the air. Skulls cracked. Blood flowed. Sharp teeth dug into the flesh of shoulders, necks, arms, and faces. Groups of beasts held down some while one attacked the face and genitals of the defenseless ones. Monsters used arms to beat others to death. Many picked up scattered stones from the initial volleys and used them against their foes. Blood, flesh, and gore were tossed into the air like confetti at a parade. It was wholesale slaughter.

Professor Biediger vomited.

Ricardo snapped another picture, then quickly prepared the camera again for another shot.

The browns regrouped when they reduced the grays to one warrior. Bodies of dead beasts littered the battlefield. The stench of hot blood and fresh death wafted into the air.

The one gray remaining, severely wounded, growled. He shouted at the browns in its primitive language, beating its chest, teeth bared.

The drums began to play a menacing beat as the crowd cheered. One huge and wounded brown stepped forward to face the gray.

Ricardo took yet another picture as Professor Biediger wiped his mouth. Then, they watched in awe.

A horn sounded, and the two warrior-beasts threw down. Punching, kicking, tearing, gouging. The two beasts ripped each other apart. Streams of blood and flesh fell from gouge wounds around their bodies, melding with the body parts of their dead kindred at their feet.

Using an advantage with speed, the gray took the browns back. He wrapped its legs around the waist of one of its foe, holding it close. He wrapped his arms around his foe's neck, then dug in with his fingers into the brown's eye sockets. The large brown cried out in pain as it flopped to the ground. It made a futile effort to defend itself, but the gray pounded and ripped at the brown until he beat him to death. Then it tore off its hanging genitals, tossing it at the remaining adversaries. The dismembered organ splashed against one of the beast's arms, splattering it with blood before splashing to the ground at their feet.

The gray then twisted the head off of the brown at its feet and held it up in triumph. The audience cheered with passion as the remaining browns knelt before the gray with an air of reverence and respect.

"Just like my *bisabuelo* said," murmured Ricardo, taking another picture. "It's some kind of ritual of power."

"Crowning a new leader, perhaps. It's got to be."

As the monsters celebrated and prepared the bodies of the slain, Professor Biediger took notes. "This will be *my* greatest discovery."

Ricardo stopped midway in preparing the camera. "*Como que* yours? This is *our* discovery. *I* told you about the legend, my family's legend. You followed it here even though you didn't believe in it. It's *ours.*"

"Oh, but you're wrong," said Biediger. "I'm just using your equipment. I paid you for its use. The pictures you took are *mine.*"

The professor smiled with a smug arrogance. "Besides, who in San Uvalde is going to believe someone like *you?*"

Ricardo suddenly burned with anger. This was *his* discovery. His father's. His grandfather's. His family's.

But before he could say anything, a large shadow passed over him. "*Ay, Dios mio,*" he muttered, looking up behind the professor.

Biediger turned around. One of the monsters towering over them. It snarled, yelling at them in the strange language. Its voice was booming. Its breath reeked, even more than its body odor that finally hit their nose.

It reached for Ricardo.

The monster's hands were massive. They held him like a child holds a doll. It shook Ricardo, whipping his neck back and forth. Its vice-like grip crushed his body. "No!" he shouted, holding up the charm.

The beast suddenly stopped. It looked him in the eyes with surprise. Then it nodded respectfully, its eyes still cold and hard.

Then it turned to Professor Biediger.

"No, I've got one, too," he cried out. "Ricardo, give it to me."

Feeling double-crossed, a part of Ricardo hope the beast would tear the professor apart. Yet, he couldn't let him be killed. There was no way he could live with that. He reached into his pocket to get the charm, but it was too late. The beast grabbed Biediger's arms and ripped them from his torso like a child snaps a dead twig from a tree. A fountain of blood spurted from the sockets as the professor cried out in agony.

Ricardo stood helpless, almost submissive, as the beast twisted the professor's head off. It popped Biediger's into its mouth and crunched on it. It then casually tossed one arm into his mouth, before stuffing the next one into his mouth, slowly pulling it into his mouth like a string of pasta.

Like a child picking up a doll off the ground, the beast picked the body off the ground and walked off. Blood poured from the exposed neck, dripping down the body and onto its large hand. It held the neck up to its mouth and squeezed Biediger's body. The corpse spat blood and gore into the beast's mouth. It chomped on it, swallowing the chewed flesh and bone. It then put the crushed carrion to its mouth and began to suck, shriveling Biediger's upper body, its innards consumed by the beast.

In a final incredible act, the flaccid upper body of Biediger was then stuffed into the monster's mouth. Tearing the corpse at the waist, it bit off the flopping torso and began chewing. As he swallowed, it took both legs in either hand, then split them like a Thanksgiving wishbone. He ate one leg, then the other, slacks and all.

Ricardo stood, shaking. He was helpless, breathless. But he was spared. Legs giving out from under him, he fell to the ground.

Looking at the earth at his knees, large footprints tracked the path where the monster walked off. Blood lined the trail.

"That's one big foot," he whispered.

He looked up at the camera and smiled. The pictures would be his, never to be made public, revealed only to his family. It was to be kept a secret like it had always been in his family. Like his grandfather wanted it.

He remembered his grandfather's words. "These monsters are cruel. They are violent, maybe even more violent than we are. And they are strong. If the world were to discover them, they would want to hunt them, to kill them like they do with all of God's creatures. They deserve a chance to live in peace, their peace, without our interference or threat from us. Because they are not like deer or birds. They are smarter, and they are stronger. Stronger than us. That is why we must leave them in peace, or risk their vengeance."

Looking down at the charm around his neck, he breathed a sigh of relief. He then looked up at the sky and made the sign of the cross.

"*Gracias, bisabuelo,*" he said. He kissed the charm his grandfather had passed down a century ago with thanks.

MATERNAL INSTINCT

BY

SHERI WHITE

*A*NY DAY NOW. *It will come any day now.*

The midwife's prediction had nearly become a prayer to Jessica by now. She couldn't wait to get home and tell Dean. Their first baby, a son, could be held as soon as tomorrow. The nursery was ready; *she* was ready. After enduring three miscarriages and seemingly endless infertility treatments, she was understandably anxious.

The light turned red.

Jessica took the opportunity to caress her huge belly, barely fitting behind the Saturn's steering wheel. As if acknowledging his mother's touch, the baby pushed against the walls of her uterus; his tiny foot was clearly visible through the flimsy fabric of her blouse. A maternal smile lit the expectant mother's face.

An impatient honk jolted her out of reverie; she glanced up at the green light, seeing thick white flakes tumble and dance in the sky. They melted on the hood of her car.

Home was still about an hour away.

Would the roads get too slick? she wondered. The snow fell harder the closer she got to home. She and Dean had purchased the converted barn and its surrounding acres during the summer and hadn't really thought about the isolation that winter could bring.

The house had captivated them immediately, capturing their hearts during the first tour of it. It had a wrap-around porch, a pot-bellied stove in the kitchen, plenty of bedroom space, storage—all the things she wanted in a house. Whenever she stepped through the kitchen door, it felt like entering a time warp to a simpler life.

She thought it was the perfect place to raise a family.

◆ ◆ ◆

The wipers whipped across the windshield, but were no match for the snow. Even with her high beams on, Jessica could only see a couple of feet ahead. Already, a few inches had fallen and she was forced to drive at a snail's pace or fear running off the sides of the road, bordered by pine trees. They bent under the snow's heavy weight.

It felt like driving through a dimly-lit tunnel.

Icy fingers of claustrophobia danced up her spine, making her shiver. The baby squirmed constantly, as if sensing his mother's anxiety.

Please just let me get home safely, Jessica thought. *I'm scared.*

She stepped on the gas just a little bit harder. This leg of the trip always made her a nervous wreck because the road became one lane, surrounded by woods. Only the locals traveled it, and not by choice. She wished Dean had gone with her to the doctor so she wouldn't be driving this road alone.

A black shape darted from the trees and into the Saturn's path. She yelled, cranking the wheel to the right and fishtailing toward the side of the road. The front tires rolled heavily over something that felt like a speed bump.

Finally, the car's front end landed in a ditch and the motor cut out. Jessica broke into tears, protectively checking her belly.

"Are you okay, little one?" she asked. "Are you okay?"

The baby gently kicked, almost reassuringly.

Jessica cried harder, simply relieved. She took deep breaths and tried to focus before attempting to start the car back up. It weakly coughed, sputtered and died.

Don't panic, she told herself. *This is why Dean bought you a cell phone.*

She reached for the tattered backpack on the passenger seat and rummaged around inside. Panic rose when she couldn't feel her phone.

Relax. Take your time.

She sifted through the junk, taking out her wallet, the most recent paperback by Nicholson and a pack of tissues. "Gah, where the hell is the stupid thing?"

Frantic, she turned the backpack upside down and dumped the rest of the stuff onto the seat next to her.

No phone.

A second later and a snapshot of the small red phone popped up still hooked to the charger on the kitchen counter, clear as day in her mind's eye. In her rush to make her appointment she must have completely forgotten it. With a cry of frustration, she swept her junk onto the floor.

Jessica wept again, laying her head on the steering wheel. *This is bad,* she thought. *I'm really in trouble.*

She leaned back against the seat and closed her eyes, trying to catch her breath and assess the situation.

Okay. She made a fist and stuck out a finger for each item she mentally counted off. *Car's stuck, won't start. No cell phone. Snow too thick to walk through, even if I wasn't nine months pregnant. On top of everything else, I could go into labor at any time.*

Crap.

Jessica's eyes flew open; panic fluttered in her chest again, making it hard to breathe.

Come on, now, Dean knows I'm due home soon. If I'm late, he'll worry. He'll probably even come after me if he can't reach me on the cell. Hopefully he'll see it sitting on the counter. Just wait a little while. His truck will come. Slightly comforted by this thought, she closed her eyes again and started to relax. Fatigued from the pregnancy, it was easy to drift off to sleep.

Nightmares could wait.

◆　◆　◆

A scraping sound, like fingernails down a chalkboard, startled Jessica awake. *What was that?*

Darkness had fallen and the blanket of snow had taken on a bluish tinge, still steadily coming down. *Must've been dreaming.* Jessica looked at her watch. 5:15.

Only about an hour had passed. She felt cold, hungry and she desperately had to pee. The baby had settled in his favorite spot, right on her bladder.

Dean should be coming any minute, she thought. *I know he will. He has to.*

Resigned to peeing on the side of the road, Jessica grabbed the door handle and started to pull.

The scratching sound returned.

Now that she was awake, she realized it was coming from the other side of the door she almost opened.

Maybe it's that poor animal I must've run over. I wonder if it's hurt?

Her maternal instincts kicked in; she gently opened the door to check the injured creature. At first glance, the creature looked like a bear cub. Its brown-black fur was matted and bloody. But what should've been its front legs looked like arms, and what should've been paws looked like misshapen, broken hands.

The creature's breathing was labored and she saw two rows of razor-sharp teeth in its mouth, below the blood oozing from its snout. Malevolent red eyes shot open, gazing into her own blue ones. It growled a deep, inhuman sound, not unlike a bear. She slammed the car door shut, muffling her screams of terror.

Please, Dean. Come find me.

The creature switched to odd mewling sounds mixed with human crying. Her heart went out to the injured creature. It didn't move.

After wrestling with her thoughts for a few minutes, she opened the door again. She tossed her coat from the back seat onto the now-unconscious animal. Hesitantly, she reached down and touched the fur on its exposed leg.

Instead of coarse hairs, the fur was soft and silky, like the flaxen hair of children. Stroking the animal's head, she felt its body shake as it forced its breathing. If she had her cell, she could call Animal Control. She didn't want the creature to die.

Reluctantly, but shivering from the cold, she shut her door and settled in to wait for her husband and the phone he would inevitably bring.

◆　◆　◆

Hours later, Jessica saw lights coming toward her. "Dean! Oh, thank God!" It seemed to take forever, but the Chevy finally stopped a few feet away from her. Jessica rolled down her window as Dean got out of the truck.

"Oh, Dean, I've been so scared," she said, starting to cry.

"Are you okay, honey? I've been worried sick about you! I saw the cell phone on the counter and when you didn't get home on time, I panicked. The doctor's office said you left hours ago. I'm so sorry, but I'm glad I found you." As he walked to the car, he stopped short. "What the hell is *that*?"

"I don't know what it is, but it's badly hurt and it growled at me. I ran over something and I'm pretty sure. . . oh, do you think I killed it?"

"I don't know. It looks like a bear, maybe a cub?" He knelt down to look the creature over.

"It's definitely not a bear. The fur feels like, I don't know, human hair, maybe. Like a baby's. It's really weird."

Dean moved her coat out of the way and put his hand on the creature's side. "It doesn't feel like it's breathing. I think it died."

Jessica's heart ached, like she had run over a neighbor's pet. "Poor thing. Dean, can we just go home now?"

"Yeah, okay. I'll call the sheriff when we get back." He stood up and reached for the door handle.

An agonized howl came from the trees, making their blood run cold.

"What was that?" Dean asked. He turned around. Jessica, too.

An obviously female creature lurched out from the trees. Her breasts hung low and heavy, dripping milky fluid.

She ran toward them, her belly as round and full as Jessica's. Black-brown fur covered her body as well.

The beast saw Dean standing over her child on the road. It screamed, saliva splattering Dean's face as the beast batted him aside like a mere doll. He flew through the air and landed face down in the snow, rolling onto his back. He moaned, unmoving.

The mother crouched down and gathered up her dead child. Gently, she rocked its body, nuzzling her cheek against the tiny face. Her sad, soft keening broke through the couple's stunned silence.

Dean pulled himself to his knees, slowly. Somehow, he managed to stand, but Jessica was worried the creature would take notice and go after him. The sound of his boots crunching through the snow seemed almost deafening. He inched his way to Jessica and the Saturn.

Before she could warn him, the beast's head whipped around. The creature put her child down on the snow with slow and gentle hands, then turned back to him. Screaming as she ran, she clawed his face, slicing the flesh to ribbons.

"Dean!" Jessica screamed. "No, please don't hurt him!" Her hands flew to her mouth; her son thrashed and kicked inside.

The mother-beast yanked Dean up by his throat. He helplessly kicked his legs in the air. He grabbed the beast's wrist in a futile effort to free himself. Her enraged eyes locked with his.

Jessica screamed. "Put him down! Oh, no. Dean!"

The creature threw Dean onto the road and fell upon him. She opened her mouth wide, filled with two rows of sharp teeth. She leaned down and in one swift bite tore out his throat completely.

Jessica let go of the urine she'd been holding in for so long and protectively clutched her stomach. Her teeth chattered and her breath hitched in horrified gasps. The mother-creature raised her head and sniffed at the air, Dean's blood dripping from her mouth.

She lumbered over to Jessica's car. Frantically, Jessica rolled up the window and locked the doors.

I'm sorry. I'm sorry, she thought, wishing she could communicate with it, *but please go away. Please, God, make her go away.*

Jessica curled up in her seat as best she could. The pungent smell of ammonia assaulted her senses, but she didn't dare open the window, even just a crack to let out the stench. Her skirt and panties were soaked, but she couldn't do anything about it.

She lowered her forehead to her drawn-up knees and softly sobbed. Everything sounded eerily quiet, but she was too afraid to look. If the thing that murdered her husband was still out there, she knew it would kill her, too. She needed to get to Dean's truck to escape, but with the monster somewhere nearby, the truck might as well have been a million miles away. She couldn't run, not in her condition. She had to check for the beast, though. She and her baby would die if she didn't make it to the truck.

Cautiously, she rolled down her window and looked around. She couldn't see anything, but she heard a low growl somewhere close by. She quickly rolled up the window. Exhausted and emotionally drained, she cried herself to sleep.

Gruesome flashes of her husband's death wove together with images of the big beast ripping her unborn son from her womb.

She awoke with a start; her back ached and her body shivered. Her coat was still outside the car door. Jessica looked around for the beast, but saw nothing. The snow had stopped and the moon peeked out from behind dark clouds. Snow sparkled and glistened in the dim moonlight. It would've been a beautiful scene if not for Dean's bloody, lifeless body sprawled on the road. She held her hands over her mouth, heaving deep, silent sobs. She averted her eyes; she couldn't think about her husband yet. Not out here. Not like this.

She opened her door a few inches, cringing as the hinges squeaked, despite her careful efforts to go slowly. The coat was barely within reach, lying beside the dead monster's baby. Why had the mother-creature left her dead child behind? She stretched her arm toward the coat, but couldn't quite get it. She grabbed the steering wheel with her right hand and leaned a little further, reaching for the coat with her left. She pulled the coat into the car when a furry black hand shot up from behind the door and yanked her wrist.

She screamed and desperately kicked at the creature's hand. As she struggled to free herself, she lost her grip on the steering wheel and accidently honked the horn. The beast roared at the noise, holding its ears and letting go of Jessica's wrist.

Breathing hard and sobbing, Jessica dropped the coat and scrambled back into the car. The door slammed hard enough to rattle the windows.

A contraction tore through her body and she screamed again, this time in pain. It squeezed her insides, making her feel as if she was in a vise. Just when she thought she might pass out from the pain, it subsided.

She leaned back in the seat, trying to catch her breath and calm down. Then her water broke.

"No! No, I can't!" she said. The water gushed from her body and streamed down her legs. Another contraction wracked her body and she moaned in terror and agony.

The mother-creature stood up immediately and peered into the car window with bloodshot eyes. The beast's eyes darkened in recognition of what was happening to her. She pounded on the window, baring her sharp teeth.

"Go away!" Jessica yelled. "Leave me alone. You killed my husband, now leave me alone!" Another contraction tore through her body, causing her belly to heave and ripple.

The mother-creature pointed at Jessica's stomach and howled.

"This is my baby!" Jessica screamed. "Mine. Now go away!" She tightly closed her eyes, retreating into the age-old childhood rule that said if you close your eyes, the monster couldn't see you.

The creature backed away from the window.

Jessica leaned back in the seat, keeping her eyes squeezed shut. *Please let labor take a long time,* she begged God or whomever would listen. *Maybe someone will come by. Maybe . . . maybe . . .*

She caressed her stomach, trying to will the baby to stay inside. The contractions continued every few minutes, but not as intensely as before. That was a good sign, she hoped.

She opened her eyes, praying the creature would be gone. She didn't see it. *Good. Maybe she went back into the woods,* she thought. She closed her eyes and took deep breaths, trying to control her fear. Pain became as overwhelming as her emotions.

◆   ◆   ◆

Jessica was able to calm down a little and opened her eyes. But then she saw Dean's body, partly covered in snow, and tears filled her eyes. It was still dark and now the moon brightly shone overhead. Her lips were dry and cracked from dehydration. She wished for a bottle of water.

Suddenly, she had an uncontrollable urge to bear down. *No. I can't have to push already. The doctor said it would take hours, maybe days of labor for a first baby.* But she had no choice. This baby was coming.

Sobbing, she took off her wet skirt and panties and threw them in the back seat. She turned around and leaned up against the door, making sure it was locked. Then she felt down between her legs.

Oh no . . .

She could feel her son's head beginning to crown. The baby would be delivered alone, with her husband's bloody body right outside her window.

Why me? How did this happen? The tears gushed anew.

A contraction hit her hard and instinctively she bore down and pushed, closing her eyes, screaming. She felt the baby's head tearing its way out. She leaned back again, waiting for the next contraction. She saw the beast staring at her from the passenger-side window. The creature pointed at Jessica's spread legs.

Jessica screamed again, more in fear than pain. She pushed once more, feeling the baby slip out of her. The mother-creature jumped up and down in excitement and beat on the window.

Jessica grabbed the baby and tightly held him to her chest. Another contraction tore through Jessica, this time expelling the placenta. The beast roared and hit the window with all her might. A crack zigzagged down the glass and the Saturn shook.

"No, stop! Please!" Jessica begged.

But Jessica's cries of terror only excited the mother-creature more. She pushed on the car, rocking it violently back and forth, almost tipping it over onto its side. Jessica's head slammed against the window, but she didn't let go of her son, who was now crying.

The beast punched the cracked window, shattering it. Her hairy hand reached for the baby, but Jessica scooted away until her back hit the other door. She knew her only chance would be to get to Dean's truck. Quickly, quietly, while the beast was trying to get in the broken window, Jessica opened the door and slipped out. She ran as fast as she could toward the truck, but she was weak and losing blood. The beast was on her only a few seconds later. Jessica felt hot pain across her back and fell to the ground. She tried to protect her baby, but the beast roughly rolled her over and grabbed him out of her arms. Jessica desperately tried to get up and rescue her son, but fell back to the ground, too weak to stand. She held out her arms and whispered "Please." The beast leaned over Jessica and roared, then sliced Jessica's throat with one swipe of her clawed hand.

The last thing Jessica saw was the creature carrying the baby into the woods. She heard her son's cries as her life slipped away.

THE FOLLOWING

BY

J. RODIMUS FOWLER

"Mary had a great big beast
Whose fleece was white as snow
And everywhere that Mary went
The beast was sure to go."

One – Hills, Eyes and the Like

Gregor had lived most of his life in the cold wastelands of Siberia. The frozen tundra that he called home was inhospitable to any but the most highly trained. He had always enjoyed the harsh environment. It gave him a feeling of accomplishment to fend for himself out there all alone. Gregor, who was a former sniper for the Soviet Army, had given up on his life of killing well before the end of the cold war. He had packed his belongings, which weren't much, and moved out into a life of bitter cold solitude. He lived off of the grid and didn't want to be found. Yet, the years had been kind to him. He had maintained his health and warmth and somehow managed to keep his belly full. All those years of training had made him a great hunter. Although he lived miles away from the nearest settlement, he often felt that something or someone was watching him. That feeling had crept over him many times over the years and there was also the matter of the missing items. Every now and then some of his tools or furs or just random things would be moved to a different location or altogether lost. Gregor tried to track down and study these strange occurrences, yet he only ever found one clue—an enormous set of foot prints in the snow. They were four times the size of his own when he stepped inside them.

Gregor was well versed in the mythology of the Sasquatch or "Yeti," as it was mostly referred to in the snowy mountain regions of Europe. He had lived in those frigid hills for a long time and never found any other evidence of them so he was fairly convinced that it was indeed simply a myth. Gregor thought maybe he had a rogue bear that wasn't afraid to get close or, at the very least, a neighboring hunter that hid his tracks well. It had been over two decades since the solitarian had fell from the views of Mother Russia and he never missed her prying eyes.

Two – Back to the Front

Six soldiers in white camouflage, led by a snarling man in a white trench coat, set out from the southeastern side of Gregor's self-proclaimed land. The loud-mouthed man was Ivan Skaarsgard, Gregor's former commander and the main reason for his drastic disappearance. Ivan was an evil, sadistic man whose only thoughts concerned death and destruction.

The soldiers reached the crest of a hill, from which they could see plumes of smoke rising from the chimney of a small cabin. The two men out front carried silenced, Kiparis 9mm submachine guns as well as Makarov 9mm pistols. The men were followed by a deadly, but beautiful woman named Lexi. She toted her specialty piece, a 9mm KASHTAN submachine gun. The fourth and fifth men in the group were the heavy hitters. They carried 7.62mm PK assault rifles, which were just lightened-up models of the dependable Kalishnikov. The sixth man in the white camouflage stayed two steps behind Ivan. This man carried his trusty machete, which never left his side, and two .45-caliber, Mexican, Obregon pistols. Miguel was the only one of the team who was not Russian. He hailed from South America and was Ivan's personal bodyguard. Ivan needed a guard, for he had screwed over many a man and country, too. He was a bloodthirsty psychopath who could not reach his fill. Over the years he had waged a private war in his head over the one that got away. Nobody walked away from him, nobody! Finally, after all these years, he had received some viable Intel on his old companion. Now it was time to pay him a visit. Gregor would soon be his and the war inside would be settled.

◆   ◆   ◆

Gregor awoke from his fleeting slumber as old ghosts ran through his head. He pulled on his thick furs and stoked the fire. It was a cold morning to say the least. He stood by the fireplace to warm himself, and stared at the former extension of his own hand that sat in place on the rack above the mantle. It was a Dragunov 7.62mm modified SVD sniper rifle; he could shoot the wings off of a flying mosquito from 300 yards with it. He lost himself in the past for just a few minutes until he heard the water on the stove begin to boil. It was coffee time.

Later, after finishing his second cup of coffee, he ventured outside to load up on firewood. It was going to be another cold, miserable day and he liked to prepare early on. He wasn't as young as he used to be. As soon as he walked outside he noticed the door of his storage building stood wide open. He walked about half way across the yard and he could already see the large imprints in the snow by the pack house. He pushed on toward the open door slowly and cautiously. There was a loud noise coming from inside the darkness. It sounded like a large man snoring, a *very* large man. Gregor noticed a strand of white fur stuck to the hinge of the open door. He reached out and grabbed it, careful to not make a sound. It smelled strongly of sweat and musk with a hint of pungent urine.

An instant later, the wood on the wall in front of his face splintered out in two small holes, followed by the *pffft-pffft* sound that imbedded itself in his mind. Silencers. Someone was shooting at him with suppressed weapons. He jumped to the ground and rolled to the side. He shuffled and kept his head down as he made his way back across the yard, chased by the steady *pffft-pffft* all around him.

About the time he made it back to the cabin and jumped through the threshold of the front door, something behind him let out a piercing roar. Gregor peeped out of the window on the left of the front door and saw a huge white beast exiting through the open door of his pack house. It stood much taller than the seven-foot door jamb. Its head was even taller than the roof line behind it. The whole beast was covered in dirty white fur. It had a massive set of arms and a dark and malicious face, which was stretched into a wicked grin as it yelped out at the world.

Gregor's heart hammered in his chest when he realized the Yeti was real.

Suddenly, automatic gunfire sounded out through the mountain skies. A thin line of bullet holes formed on the wall of the pack house to the left of the raging beast. Then the holes moved across the wall toward the beast and right across its midsection. The Yeti let out another howl, one of pain this time instead of rage. The creature ran straight out into the yard and must have spotted one of the shooters because Gregor saw its eyes change direction and home in on something before darting off in that direction. Gregor strapped on a couple of his heaviest furs, grabbed all the ammo he could tote, and took the Dragunov from its resting place over the mantle. It was time to get the heck out of Dodge.

Three – Hunter and the Prey

Ivan, Lexi and Miguel were further toward the back of the assault. They heard the sounds it made and that in itself unsettled their nerves. Ivan moved closer and saw one of his soldiers unload his 9mm submachine gun into the stomach of a giant white creature at close range; it never even slowed the creature down. The beast grabbed the man in the white camouflage and ripped his arm from his body with one swift pull. The one armed man took the handgun out of its holster with his remaining hand and shot the creature between the eyes point-blank. A thin red wound appeared in the fur on the beast's head. The creature screamed and lifted the man into the air above its head then slammed him to the ground head first. The man never moved again.

Another man in white camouflage rushed the creature from behind, quickly unloading his submachine gun into the beast's lower back.

◆　◆　◆

From the back corner of the cabin, Gregor watched the scene unfold. He looked through the scope of his Dragunov. A jolt of surprise ran through him when the Yeti emerged from the pack house. He saw Ivan Skaarsgard and his ex-lover Lexi Wrenn.

"What are they doing here?" he said.

Not believing it yet not opposing it either, he took aim through his beloved rifle and sent a single 7.62mm round out across the snowy field. The round struck its target with pinpoint accuracy. The man behind the creature, shooting it in the back, fell to the ground, making a bloody mess in the snow. The Yeti looked back toward the cabin and roared at the top of its lungs then turned its attention back to the soldiers at hand. The heavy hitters fired at the creature from opposing sides with their assault rifles; the Yeti was hardly slowed down. It made its way closer to one of the soldiers, but the gunman on the other side was relentless and kept firing.

Gregor took aim again and released another round. He shot the man on the left side of the beast directly in the temple, sending his brains spraying out the opposite side of his head. The Yeti scooped up the remaining soldier as he turned his back to run away. The beast pulled the man close and squeezed him with all of its might, then dropped the broken man's corpse onto the snow at its feet. It raised its hands up above its head and pounded its chest like an ape, howling with primal rage.

◆　◆　◆

Lexi was about twenty yards in front of Ivan and his elite bodyguard. She wasn't looking back, this time running away. Ivan retreated toward the trucks as well, with his Latin shadow right behind. The woman turned and made it to the cover of the forest instead.

Ivan looked over his shoulder and shouted, "You better get me outta this, Miguel! I'll double your salary!"

Miguel, who had both of his .45 caliber Obregons in hand, just looked at Ivan and winked. Ivan knew the man never had any respect for him—he was simply an employer to Miguel—but he did have a greed that couldn't be satisfied and that kept Miguel close.

Ivan looked around for Lexi and couldn't see her. He hoped she had found cover. Hands trembling, he fumbled with his satellite phone and dropped it before he could send the call. He dove to the ground and snatched the phone from the wet snow before it was rendered useless. He sent the call and impatiently waited for the voice on the other end to answer.

He was mumbled to himself, "Come on, come on, come on . . ."

A shot came straight through the satellite phone and took two of Ivan's fingers with it. Ivan yelped, but being the efficient soldier her was, quickly grabbed his sleeve and yanked a piece of fabric from his coat and wrapped it around the wound. When he looked back up, Miguel was nowhere to be seen. Ivan pulled out his Makarov 9mm and looked out across the vast white wilderness. He streamlined back to the truck to make his escape and to use the other satellite phone.

Now Ivan was alone and furious, but he still stood on his own two feet. He ran a short ways through the snow before kneeling down on one knee. He heard the loud scream behind him. The creature was near. Ivan crawled for the tree line off to the right. Every time his weight crushed the untouched snow it made a loud crunching sound that echoed inside his head. He wished he had gotten through to back-up, but it was too late for that. He heard the thunderous footsteps coming up behind him; he dove into the darkness of the forest, sliding up next to the nearest large tree. Through the brush, Ivan saw the creature cautiously step up to the edge of the forest, its head tilted slightly to the left, apparently listening.

Just behind the beast, Miguel came out from his hiding spot underneath the snow and fired at the furry creature in the back and sides. As soon as he emptied the first nine rounds into the beast, he placed one of the pistols back on his side and retrieved his machete. The Yeti turned around fast and swung its mighty arm at him. The South American dodged the first attack and countered with his blade, slicing it deep into the creatures arm. The creature immediately lashed out with its uninjured arm and knocked Miguel back to the snow.

Ivan stood from his hiding spot to get a better view.

The beast dove on top of Miguel with its enormous feet and began to stomp him into the frozen ground. Ivan shot the creature in the back of the head and kept on firing until his pistol was empty. The Yeti slowly turned around and pulled the machete from its arm. It threw the blade into the woods and the shiny metal disappeared in the trees. Ivan turned and ran toward where he thought the trucks were. The creature let out a mighty roar and followed the commander. About every third step or so Ivan fell to the ground and quickly picked himself up, only to repeat the process several more times.

◆ ◆ ◆

A safe distance away, Gregor watched as the Yeti swiftly made his way to Ivan, who was now on his knees looking up at the massive beast. Gregor looked through his scope in an attempt to read the man's lips, and pieced together what the Russian was saying—He was calling out for Lexi. The Sasquatch raised its enormous feet and viciously stomped Ivan into the ground. The war inside the psychopath's head was finally over.

A tree limb cracked from further up the mountain. The Yeti turned his head to the trees and locked his eyes on something then set out in that direction. Gregor panned his scope around to the forest and saw Lexi running for her life. He followed them both.

Lexi ran to the clearing on the other side of the dense forest. The trucks were parked there. As soon as she was about three car lengths away from the closest truck, Gregor fired at the vehicle. It exploded into a ball of fire, knocking her to the ground. She slowly got up and ran past the burning vehicle, trying and make it to the next one in line. Another shot, and the black Land Rover also exploded into a huge ball of flame. A piece of shrapnel from the explosion lodged itself into her shoulder and she felt back to the frozen ground again. This time she equipped her special KASHTAN submachine gun with her good arm and waited for the Yeti to get closer.

Gregor saw Lexi through his scope; she waved up to the woods where he was hiding. Then she pointed her gun at the face of the looming creature. A second later, Gregor put her out of her misery, one final clean kill. The Yeti turned and looked to the forest, to the same spot where he stood. It let out a fierce roar and beat its hands against its chest. Gregor raised his Dragunov high into the air and fired off the last two rounds in the clip. The shots echoed through the mountains. The two hunters locked eyes for a brief moment. The Yeti turned around and slowly walked away until it was no longer visible. The white fur blended in with the frozen landscape. Gregor turned and retraced his steps back to his cabin. He walked to the pack house and shut the door. Inside, he put on a pot of boiling water. It was soon to be coffee time.

THE YETI HUNTERS

BY

PAUL A. FREEMAN

JEREMY SUTTON, PROFESSOR of Anthropology at Easthampton University, was enjoying a full English breakfast in spite of his doctor's advice to avoid red meat and fatty foods, when he heard an envelope slide through the letterbox. Out of habit he looked up at the kitchen clock. He frowned. It was only eight-forty-three, too early for the regular postal delivery. Curiosity soon got the better of him. He put down his knife and fork and went to investigate. As he reached the front porch of his modest, semi-detached house, outside a car accelerated away.

On the doormat lay an A4 manila envelope. His name was printed in large capital letters on the front. There was no address beneath his name—so he assumed it had been hand delivered—and there was no return address on the back.

More inquisitive than ever, Sutton tore open the envelope. Inside was a grainy, twelve-by-eight, black-and-white photograph. His excitement rising at the subject of the photograph, he turned the picture over. A mobile phone number was scrawled on the reverse side. He dialled it immediately.

"Hello? To whom am I speaking?" he said.

"Tracey."

"Tracey Eldridge? Professor Eldridge's daughter?"

"That's right."

"I haven't seen you since you were a teenager. It's been a while."

"Yes, it has!" There was an awkward silence before Tracey rhetorically asked, "Do you have the photograph I left you?"

"I do." Sutton looked down at the picture. A hairy, long-armed creature was lumbering up a snow-covered mountain slope. "Have you considered it could be another hoax? How much did your father pay for *this* yeti photograph?"

"He didn't pay anything. He took it himself."

There was a moment of stunned silence before Sutton asked, "Why deliver the picture to me? As I recall, Professor Eldridge isn't in the habit of sharing his finds—genuine *or* fake—with his rivals."

"That's because you and your academic ilk treat my father like a kook, like some nutty professor who's lost the plot. You think he's obsessive, that he's to be pitied rather than taken seriously." She drew a deep breathe, then, putting aside Sutton's criticism of her father's professional integrity, continued: "He entrusted me with half a dozen yeti pictures on a memory card. They were taken above the Himalayan snowline, on the Gokyo Plateau during our last expedition, while I remained at base camp due to altitude sickness and my leg."

Sutton recalled one of Eldridge's earlier yeti expeditions. A fall into a crevasse left Tracey with multiple fractures to her femur and a permanent limp.

"I don't see how I come into all this," he said.

"When Dad and his Sherpa, Dilup, went back up to the plateau to further explore the yetis' habitat, he told me I was to contact you if anything happened to them. Despite your hostility toward my father's theories on yeti colonies, he admires your professional objectivity. So, now that I've got your undivided attention, if you're interested in seeing the other pictures, pop on over to Eldridge House."

Thirty minutes later, having abandoned his half-finished breakfast for the cleaning lady to clear up, Sutton arrived at his contemporary anthropologist's family mansion.

Tracey Eldridge met him at the door. Now in her mid-thirties, her smooth, youthful face had become lined by the worries of adulthood, whilst her cute grin had transformed into a rigid, unsmiling grimace. As she led Sutton to Professor Eldridge's study, Sutton noted the swivelling limp to her gait.

With a magnifying glass he examined the photographs Tracey had tempted him with. Some, taken at a distance, showed a "yeti" ascending the rocky, snow-laden slopes leading to Nepal's Gokyo Plateau. Others were of artefacts, stone axes and flint spearheads, the day-to-day tools of highly evolved hominids. The final picture showed the smouldering embers of a rudimentary campfire.

Declaring the pictures almost certainly genuine, Sutton sat for a moment in dazed disbelief. "Incredible! These creatures may be descended from the sub-species which evolved into *homo sapiens*. Look! They use stone tools and fire, just as our Stone Age ancestors did."

"Father's of the same opinion. He believes yetis are the missing link between modern man and lesser simians."

"Where is Peter?" Sutton asked. He looked about the study as if his anthropological competitor might be lurking in the shadows, smugly grinning at being vindicated after so many years. "I must congratulate him on this unique discovery."

Tracey produced a last photograph. It showed her father and a grinning Sherpa in climbing garb.

"I took this picture when father and Sherpa Dilup returned from their preliminary reconnoitre of the plateau. They were beside themselves with excitement. As I said, they then entrusted me with the yeti pictures and went back up the mountain to secure artefacts, some physical proof of the yetis' existence to satisfy the likes of you. That was the last I, or anyone else, has seen of them. It's also another reason I contacted you. I need your help to find out what happened to my father. I want to mount an expedition in utmost secrecy to avoid it becoming a circus."

Sutton opened his mouth intending to decline Tracey's offer. Yet the words that came out, fuelled by the prospect of worldwide renown, were anything but a refusal. "Of course I'll help you find Peter," he said, dreaming of the recognition a *bona fide* missing link would bring him.

A week later, in a Twin Otter airplane, Professor Sutton and Tracey Eldridge flew from Kathmandu to the small Himalayan settlement of Lukla. Thinness of the air, changeable weather conditions, and a sloping runway surrounded on the one side by cliffs and on the other by a sheer drop meant Lukla arguably boasted the world's most dangerous airport.

As the aircraft approached the runway, Tracey gripped the armrests of her seat until her knuckles stood out white. Sutton, however, noticed nothing of their perilous surroundings, absorbed as he was in Professor Peter Eldridge's popular paperback, *Abominable Snowman: Myth or Reality*.

He had been reading about how, in Nepal, the yeti was referred to as "rakshasa," meaning "demon," or "JoBran," meaning "man-eater," and that some thought the beast was descended from a race of giant apes, the *giantophitecus*, which migrated to the Himalayas half a million years ago.

The evidence tantalised him—huge footprints of an inconclusive nature; blurry photographs of what appeared to be a large, hairy biped; documentation of a pre-Buddhist era god of hunting, an apelike creature known as "The Glacier Being," which communicated through whistling sounds and carried rocks as weapons.

After two days acclimatising to the altitude at Nanche Bazaar, the last sizable settlement before entering the high Himalayas, Professor Sutton and Tracey Eldridge began their trek to the Gokyo Plateau. Because of Tracey's leg they arranged for supplies to be helicoptered to a rocky outcrop high above the well-stocked Eldridge Expedition base camp rather than carry the load themselves.

They were in for a shock though, when they arrived at base camp. Nestling in the forests below the Himalaya Mountains, the cabin had been virtually demolished, its supplies scattered about the forest floor or stolen.

"Bloody hippy trekkers," said Tracey. "They've trashed the place."

Sutton was not so sure trekkers were to blame. "Look at that." He pointed to scratches on one of the two wooden walls still standing. "Don't those look like claw marks to you?"

Tracey nodded. "And they're too high up to have been made by a bear." She took out her camera. "Whatever made these marks must be at least ten feet tall."

They spent the night huddled in a lean-to constructed from the remains of the cabin. Yet they got little sleep, for whatever ripped the expedition base camp apart was still out there in the Himalayan forests or the mountains beyond.

At first light the next morning they set off for their final assault on the Gokyo Plateau, Professor Eldridge's last known location.

Several hours into the climb, above the snowline and panting due to the high altitude, Sutton said, "We can guess from your father's photographs and from what happened to the cabin that the yetis come down regularly to the upper reaches of the Himalayan forests, probably to gather firewood and forage for food."

"What do you suppose they eat?" Tracey asked, unease inflected in her voice.

Sutton shrugged. "Snow foxes, honey bears, yaks—whatever they can find, I suppose. That's if they use the firewood they collect for cooking and not just to keep warm. Otherwise they may subsist on nuts and berries. It's very intriguing."

"What are the chances Father's still alive?"

"Peter lived amongst Greenland's Inuits for several months under extreme conditions," said Sutton. "If these yetis are as evolved as they appear to be, perhaps he's staying at their encampment learning about their culture, their language even, if they've got one."

Tracey did not look too hopeful. "Climbers disappear all the time on the Gokyo Plateau. The area's renowned for the instability of its snow shelves and frequent avalanches. Last year alone five climbers went missing. None of their bodies were ever recovered."

In an uneasy silence, roped together for safety, the duo trudged on through the snow. As the drifts deepened, Tracey struggled more and more because of her game leg. Each time she extricated herself from the snow, Sutton paused and anxiously glanced up at the precarious snow-and-ice overhangs surrounding them.

At mid-afternoon a whooping noise abruptly cut through the crisp quietness of the Himalayan air.

"Yetis!" hissed Tracey. She laboured against the thin atmosphere to catch up with Sutton.

The whooping sounded again. Sutton searched the distant ridgelines with his binoculars. Something moved on the periphery of his vision, but by the time he trained the lenses on it, the object had gone.

"There's nothing up there," he informed his companion. "Perhaps it's just the supply helicopter we can hear."

Tracey nodded, but there was little conviction in the gesture.

Uneasy though they felt, they toiled upwards toward a treacherous-looking snow shelf beneath the Gokyo Plateau. Suddenly the whooping started up again, louder this time. It echoed and resounded around the encircling mountains until it was replaced by an ominous rumbling.

"Avalanche!" Tracey screamed, as sections of the ice shelf above them broke away.

Whether due to the instinct for self-preservation, or a scientist's natural aversion to sharing credit for a discovery, Sutton pulled out his climber's knife. Moments later he cut the rope, freeing himself from his disabled climbing partner. He moved off as quickly as he could perpendicular to the direction of the avalanche. His efforts were futile though, and within seconds a tumbling tide of whiteness swept both him and the companion he had ruthlessly abandoned off their feet.

Disoriented, encased in a frigid tomb, Sutton listened without much hope for any noises presaging rescue. However, all he heard was his own laboured breath and the rush of blood pumping round his body from a stressed heart. He pushed against the walls of what he assumed would prove to be his grave, compacting the snow and giving himself a little breathing space.

Trapped and helpless, his mind raced. He had visions of snowfall, year by year, compressing the weight of the snow above him until it formed a glacier, a river of ice that would flow from the upper reaches of the Himalayas into the valley below. He saw himself centuries from now staring out of a glassy-blue glacier snout while curious trekkers stared in at his frozen, perfectly-preserved corpse, wondering who this poor devil was.

Professor Sutton's morbid reverie was interrupted by the end of a stick prodding his shoulder. At first, in his confused, oxygen-starved state, he did not realise its significance. Then, as the stick poked him in the back he gave silent thanks.

The avalanche probe jabbed him for a third time on the back of the leg and gave way to scratching and scraping sounds from above. Dim sunlight penetrated the layers of snow and ice entombing him and he pictured the supply helicopter's crew desperately digging to free him before he succumbed to hyperthermia.

A circle of blue sky finally appeared above him, dug out not by a steel snow spade, but by a primitively-carved wooden shovel. The next moment strong, furry arms, longer than any ape's, plucked him from his ice-cold crypt.

His eyes widened in horror. Instead of an aircrew, his rescuers were three monsters—a trio of snarling yetis. Standing twelve feet tall, one carried the wooden shovel and the long, thin stick which had been used as an avalanche probe. The other two, armed with clubs, communicated in a rudimentary language consisting of whistles, grunts and growls. Their naked, long-limbed bodies were covered with thick white hair and their overhanging brows were creased in thought as if deciding what to do with this interloper.

"El-drij," one of the yetis grunted, moving menacingly forward and motioning toward Sutton with its club. "El-drij."

"Eldridge? That's my father!"

Sutton spun round to find Tracey, newly rescued from the avalanche by a second group of yetis. The sheer suddenness of her voice coupled with the shock of seeing real, live yetis made his legs give way, sending him to his knees.

She spoke between gasps and was shivering with cold. "Dad must be alive!" she said, her pale face suddenly infusing with a ruddy, optimistic glow. "You heard what this creature said. He's alive!"

Rather than being afraid, Tracey seemed galvanised with excitement. Yet when Sutton observed her more closely he noticed the narrow scowl of accusation in her eyes. It made him speculate on how the world would react to news of him cutting the lifeline between himself and a crippled woman. He wondered whether he could live with the shame of what he had done if it became common knowledge; he concluded his career would be over. There was time to dwell on his cowardly actions later, however. Until then he had to deal with the precarious yeti situation. These primitive creatures could kill him out of hand, so to survive he had to fall back on his anthropological expertise.

"El-drij," the yeti repeated. He urgently pointed at Sutton, then upwards toward the looming Gokyo Plateau.

"I reckon they must have trapped your father and Dilup in the same manner they trapped us," Sutton said. His heart still beat hard, quick. He could only assume Tracey's was doing the same, adrenaline rushing through her system. "They probably used the resonance of their cries to set off an avalanche. Peter and his Sherpa must be up on the plateau at the yetis' settlement. Imagine what your father's learned about these creatures if he's been living with them all this time."

Prodded by the yetis' clubs and urged on by their constant repetition of the word "El-drij," Professor Sutton and Tracey climbed the steep, rocky incline leading to the plateau. Realising the importance of demonstrating his strength and resilience, Sutton spurned the loping creatures' helping hands, whilst Tracey, having stumbled to her knees several times, bore the indignity of being carried by the yeti leader, slung over his shoulder in a fireman's lift.

"I can smell a wood fire," said Tracey when they arrived at the yetis' encampment and she was finally put down.

Her teeth chattering, she told Sutton she was going to warm herself up for a minute or two. However, before she could locate the fire, the yeti leader said, "El-drij," and pointed to a cave entrance set in a mountainside behind a sprawl of primitive lean-tos.

She and Sutton moved toward the cave, but the yetis blocked Tracey's path, leaving the way for the professor unobstructed.

"For some reason they seem willing only to admit me," said Sutton, and with a resigned shrug entered the cave along with the yeti leader.

Professor Sutton's eyes took time adjusting to the gloom, but finally he perceived a human figure propped up by the wall in a chamber at the far end of the cavern. He drew near, and on closer inspection the mysterious shape resolved itself into the frozen, emaciated corpse of Professor Peter Eldridge. The man's hair was grizzled, dusted with frost, and he wore an unkempt beard.

"El-drij," said the yeti, affectionately patting the dead man's head. "Tea-cher!"

"Eldridge was your teacher?" asked Sutton incredulously.

"One, two, three, four!" the creature replied by way of confirmation. Then, standing back and taking in Professor Sutton's comparable age and appearance—what with Sutton's stubbly beard and uncombed hair—the yeti added, "Now you tea-cher. New El-drij."

Sutton was about to protest, but appreciated that his very survival might rest on replacing Professor Eldridge as the yetis' teacher. Seemingly, the word "El-drij" had become a generic term in the yeti community—probably something akin to "Wise One" or "Knowledge Giver"—and the similarity between his and Peter Eldridge's appearance had singled him out as the yetis' next wise knowledge giver. Until an opportunity of escape presented itself, instructing these beasts in the basics of English and showing them how to fashion primitive tools from pieces of wood would be a small price to pay for staying alive.

Sutton's only immediate concern was that Peter Eldridge's emaciated body indicated the scientist had died from starvation. *Why,* he wondered, *did my fellow anthropologist fail to sustain himself? Is the yeti diet so inedible? Did* they *starve him?*

As if understanding Sutton's anxiety, the yeti leader took him to an even darker part of the cave. It was strewn with climbing equipment and torn clothing. Sutton frowned and picked up a tattered shirt. He discovered the tears in it were made by claws and the material was stained with blood. Recalling what Tracey had said about trekkers and climbers disappearing in the vicinity, he tossed the shirt back on the ground in revulsion. Yet as he did so, he noticed a more substantial object amongst this detritus of the dead. Squinting into the darkness, he discerned the gutted torso and attached head of Sherpa Dilup.

The yeti pointed to the human remains. "Food!" he said.

Appalled, Sutton staggered toward the cave entrance, stopping only to vomit against the wall. At last he realised the truth. The yetis were carnivores. The avalanches they triggered were a means for acquiring food. They were the hunters, the unwary trekkers and climbers their prey. What Tracey had taken to be the yetis' campfire was in fact a cooking fire. It meant Professor Eldridge, although he had taught the yetis— probably whilst biding his time in hopes of escape—had chosen a long, lingering death by starvation rather than submitting to cannibalism.

Stumbling from what was in effect a food larder hollowed out of the rock, Sutton emerged into the open. Breathing hard, he fell to his knees and looked out over a murmuring crowd of yetis. Somewhere in their midst Tracey shouted to him, "What about my father? Did you speak to him? Is he alive?"

Sutton sensed the yeti leader shambling up behind him and once more the instinct for self-preservation asserted itself. If it was a matter of life and death, his life and death, then he had to put any qualms about cannibalism behind him, and become the yetis' Knowledge Giver. But what to do about Tracey? She could ruin him if the truth of how he survived this ordeal ever became public.

Ignoring Tracey's desperate enquiries about her father, Professor Jeremy Sutton patted his chest. "Tea-cher," he announced to the expectant yetis, accepting the mantel of their new "El-drij," their new Knowledge Giver. Then, to remove the one witness who could testify on the lengths he went to survive, he pointed with a trembling finger toward Tracey.

"Food!" he said, his voice quavering. "Food!"

The yeti directly behind Tracey immobilised her in an arm lock and deftly twisted her head until her neck snapped.

A few hours later, after taking the pragmatic course of action and forcing a few morsels of roasted Sherpa down his throat and having seen Tracey and Professor Eldridge's gutted carcases added to the larder, Sutton watched with a professional anthropologist's eye as the yetis went about their daily business.

That night, his conscience clear in spite of breaking man's greatest taboo, Professor Sutton dreamed of the fame and fortune awaiting him when he brought news of a yeti colony back to the civilised world.

FRESH MEAT

BY

REBECCA BESSER

SAMUEL YODER WALKED out to his barn in the velvety, violet dark just before dawn. As he came closer to the large red and white structure, he noticed the barn door was partially open and he heard his cows lowing in distress. Increasing his pace, he rushed forward and went inside. He held his oil lantern high, almost above his head, and peered into the gloom, trying to see what had distressed his animals.

Dark red blood and chunks of flesh were strewn about and mixed in with the golden hay that covered the wooden floor boards. For a moment Samuel was shocked to the point his mind couldn't process what he was seeing. The scene before him was ripe with violent bloodshed. Shaking with fear, he advanced into the barn, following the blood trail, looking for the source of the carnage. He stopped at every stall and made sure each animal was all right. It wasn't until he came close to the back of the barn that he found what he was looking for.

Bessie's—his prize Brown Swiss—stall was coated in dripping wet, fresh blood. Her hooves and legs lay at oddly grotesque angles, her rib cage broken and torn apart. Her intestines had slipped from her body cavity to lay raw and colorful in the hay. Her head was completely missing and, judging by the way the flesh around the top of the neck was folded and wrinkled, it looked like someone had twisted it until it popped off.

Samuel couldn't think of anything big enough, or strong enough, to rip a cow's head clean off.

With hands shaking so hard he feared he might drop the lantern, he hung it on a peg by the stall gate. He didn't want to burn down the barn on top of losing his prize cow. Slowly, he walked into the stall and looked around; expecting to see Bessie's dead, lifeless eyes staring at him from one of the corners, but her head was nowhere to be found.

He carefully examined the stall, looking for clues as to what might have done this; he could tell by the carnage that it wasn't done by man, despite the large hand prints on the wall that looked human. They were far too big to be a man's.

"Da?" a young female voice called from the entrance to the barn. "Where are you?"

Just as Samuel turned, he saw his seven-year-old daughter round the corner for a full view of Bessie's remains. She screamed.

"Rachel!" Samuel exclaimed, rushing forward, tripping over one of the almost-severed cow legs. He fell hard with a loud squish in the middle of Bessie's stomach, breaking open the digestive compartments. Blood and half-digested grass and hay shot out to the immediate area, covering Rachel's little face and brown dress with slime. She screamed louder in horror and disgust. He reached out to her, but he could tell from the vacant look in her eyes that she'd already gone into shock.

◆　　◆　　◆

Four miles away, Joshua Troyer climbed the steps onto the school bus just as the first rays of dawn were cresting over the tree-tops on the horizon. He was the first one picked up and the last one to be dropped off on the bus' route, which meant he spent an extra hour riding each way. He hated living in the rural area his parents had bought a house in, but they loved the peace and quiet, and his father had grown up here. He thought it was boring and couldn't see how anything fun or interesting could ever happen in an out-of-the-way place like Coshocton County, Ohio, but his dad had taken a job with the railroad and they'd had to move away from Chicago, much to his lament.

He walked to his preferred seat at the back of the bus and made himself comfortable, slipping in his ear-buds so he could listen to his MP3 player and hopefully go back to sleep.

Josh was just drifting off when he heard Mrs. Crowley—the bus driver—scream at the top of her lungs. He felt a thump like the bus had hit something, and then the bus swayed as it swerved back and forth on the narrow township road.

He flew out of his seat sideways.

"What the heck?" he exclaimed and tried to get up off the floor. He was finally able to stand when the bus came to a sudden, screeching halt. "What happened? What'd you hit?"

Mrs. Crowley had stopped screaming and was now staring; mouth agape, at a cow who peered in at her from the hood.

Josh walked up the aisle to the front of the bus. "Holy cow!" he said with a half-smirk at his pun.

Sitting on the hood of the bright yellow school bus was the decapitated head of a tanish-brown cow. Blood ran in red rivers down both sides of the bus, dripping off the fenders and onto the blacktop road.

"Sweet," he said. "Where did that come from?"

Mrs. Crowley didn't answer, but stared at the head on the hood, gripping the steering wheel for dear life.

Josh reached forward and opened the bus' door and started down the stairs, but only made it to the second one; something large slammed into the back of the bus hard enough to rock it. Mrs. Crowley cried out, but her eyes remained transfixed on the severed bovine head. He stepped back up into the bus and peered down the rows of seats and out the back window, expecting to see a car or truck that had rear-ended the bus, but there was no vehicle. With a shrug he faced the stairs again and moved to descend when suddenly a huge, hairy arm reached in and grabbed his ankle, yanking it out from under him. He fell back onto the hard, black, rubber-matted floor of the bus with a loud, painful *thud*.

Screaming, with his heart racing in panic, he lashed out with his legs and tried to get free of the shackling hand, but the grip was too tight. It tugged again, rougher this time, and Josh reached out for something to hold onto as the face belonging to the arm came into view.

Deep-set, dark eyes looked at him from a face completely covered in thick, almost black, hair. The mouth of the creature was open wide, baring fangs and spraying thick, blood-laced spittle in a deafening roar that broke Mrs. Crowley's stupor, making her scream again.

"Help!" Josh yelled, looking up at the bus driver, but she didn't make any move to assist him.

He kicked out at the creature and noticed that its entire body was covered with the same hair as its face. He managed to kick hard enough, and at the right angle, to pinch the monster's knuckles between the metal frame of the door and his foot, causing the creature to lose its grip for a moment.

Josh lunged forward and grabbed the handle to close the door and almost had it shut when the arm shot back in and grabbed his foot. It tugged hard and Josh wiggled, slipped off his sneaker, which was quickly pulled outside and then thrown at the closed door in frustration.

Breathing heavily, Josh rose to his feet and backed away from the door, jumping when he came into contact with Mrs. Crowley, who was still gripping the steering wheel, but was now focused on the giant, hairy monster just outside the bus door. It roared with fury and beat on the door with its fists, bending the metal frames slightly and cracking the glass. When it wasn't able to breach the barrier, it looked for another way in, leaping up onto the hood and knocking the cow's head off with its giant foot.

The creature pressed its face against the windshield and stared at them, its breath fogging the window as it panted with apparent excitement. It grinned suddenly and sat back on the hood—holding itself steady with its hands pressed to the hood behind its back—and started kicking the windshield.

"Bigfoot . . ." Josh muttered, staring as the huge foot of the monster slammed again and again into the safety glass.

Mrs. Crowley started screaming louder, and drew Josh's attention. Glancing swiftly back and forth between her and Bigfoot, he knew they had to do something fast or they'd be served as dessert after the main course of cow brains.

"Drive the bus!" he screamed, shaking her. "If you don't get us out of here it's going to kill us!"

Something he said penetrated the bus driver's shock and panic, because she took off with a jerk, sending Bigfoot sliding off the hood. It flipped in midair and landed on its feet as they speed off into the early morning mist. The beast ran after them for a moment, but turned back, collected the cow head, and disappeared into the dark shadows of the forest when it probably realized it wouldn't be able to keep up.

"It's gone," Josh breathed. "It went into the woods."

Mrs. Crowley didn't say anything; she just kept driving, whimpering every now and again, passing all the houses she was supposed to stop at and pick up the children.

"Where are we going?" Josh asked.

She didn't respond.

He sat down on the seat directly behind her, ignoring his missing shoe, and hoped she'd get them wherever they were going safely.

◆ ◆ ◆

"What do you mean your bus was attacked by Bigfoot?" Josh's mom asked when she came to pick him up an hour later. "There's no such thing as Bigfoot. Is that the best excuse you can come up with for losing your shoe? Really? Couldn't you think up something more believable?"

"Yes, there is!" Josh said. *I wonder if every fifteen-year-old has parents that don't believe anything they say?* He thought and rolled his eyes. "Really, Mom,

Bigfoot attacked our bus. He was carrying around the head of a cow, and he tried to rip me out of the bus and took my shoe! It's probably still lying by the road from when he threw it and it bounced off the bus."

She frowned. "It was probably someone dressed up in a costume, pranking everyone."

"Really?" he asked, sarcasm lacing his tone. "Then they need to see a dentist, have a good shave, and stop taking steroids, because it was one messed up prankster. You should see what Bigfoot did to the bus!"

With a heavy sigh, his mom rubbed her forehead with the fingertips of both hands and closed her eyes. "Josh . . . I don't want to argue about this right now. I came to take you home because the school called. You have to have a psychological evaluation before you'll be allowed to return. The principal thinks you might be suffering from some kind of delusions because of your fantastical tale. Now get in the car."

Josh stood where he was, not moving even an inch closer to the car. He pointed over his shoulder with his thumb. "You want to see the bloody, broken bus? Or stop by the hospital and talk to Mrs. Crowley?"

"No, I don't!" his mom screamed. "I want you to get in the car so we can go home. I think this is a really crappy thing to make up just because you don't like living here. I've called your father and he'll have to miss work to come and have a talk with the principal to straighten this out. I'm not happy."

Josh, finally giving in to defeat, shrugged and hobbled—because of his missing shoe and uneven gait—over to the car. He wrenched the door open and got in, slamming the door closed behind him. After buckling his seat-belt he stared straight ahead and didn't say another word the entire way home. When they arrived, he ran into the house, went to his room, and slammed and locked the door.

He paced for five minutes and decided he would have to come up with a plan to prove he hadn't lied. He knew his dad wouldn't believe him either. Heck, the principal and his mom hadn't believed him, so why should his dad?

Busy, working on a plan, not coming out of his room no matter how much his parents pleaded with him or threatened him with punishments, he skipped dinner and waited for his parents to go to bed.

◆　◆　◆

The sun was setting and Samuel was pulling his buggy into his hard-packed dirt driveway. The horse, knowing it was home, picked up its pace and pulled them swiftly to the house. Rachel lay between Samuel and Hannah on the hard bench seat. She was sleeping peacefully, finally.

"Whoa, Samson," Samuel called softly to the horse, pulling back on the reins. "Do you want me to carry her into the house?" he asked his wife.

Hannah nodded, and he stepped down from the buggy before lifting Rachel into his arms. Her white cap was coming loose and it hung at an odd angle from her head. They'd changed her clothes earlier before they'd taken her to the doctor, from the brown one to a dark blue one; it was wrinkled from traveling. As he was mounting the porch steps, their son Elijah came out to greet them, carrying the shotgun Samuel used for deer hunting.

"I cleaned up the barn, as you asked, Father," he said anxiously, fidgeting with the barrel of the gun as he sat it down and leaned the muzzle against the wooden porch railing. "How's Rachel? What did the doctor say?"

"When I return, Elijah," Samuel said, with a grim expression as he passed his teenage son and went into the house. His wife followed him, but not before eyeing the shotgun with a grimacing.

Samuel carried his sleeping daughter upstairs to her room, where Hannah pulled back the homemade quilt that covered Rachel's bed so he could lay her down. They stood, looking down at their sleeping child for a long time before Hannah broke the silence.

"Maybe we *should* contact the police," she whispered desperately, glancing at her husband. "What if whatever killed Bessie comes back? What if it attacks one of the children next time?"

Samuel looked at his wife and sighed. "It will be as God wills it. We will defend ourselves the best we can against whatever beast it was that did this; I'm thinking it was a bear. Other than that, there is nothing we can do." He turned and left the room.

He paused in the hallway and glanced back. The sight of Hannah wiping tears from her cheeks as she undressed Rachel caused his heart to ache. He was doing what he thought best for his family, and he hoped his wife understood. With a heavy sigh, he continued down the hall and to the stairs, praying for God's guidance to keep his family safe.

◆　◆　◆

Josh snuck out of his room and went to the hall closet where he knew the digital video camera was kept. As quietly as he could, he gathered the camera and checked the black case it was stored in to make sure there was an extra battery. Carrying it back to his room, he sat it on his bed while he slid into a black hoodie that matched his black jeans and dark boots. His plan was simple: get video proof that Bigfoot existed. He didn't even think it might be an impossibility. After all, people had been trying for years to get a glimpse of the hairy beast, but with no success. He never doubted for one second he would get the footage he wanted. He'd seen Bigfoot in the flesh and knew where his trail was.

Sneaking out was easier than he'd thought it would be, even without the background noise of traffic he'd grown up with. He'd been scared he would knock something over and alert his parents to his activity, but he'd made it out of the house like a ninja.

As he walked down the blacktopped road, the silence and blackness of the world around him was eerie and disconcerting. This was the first time he'd been out at night by himself since they'd moved to Coshocton. The weak flashlight he'd brought with him only lit an area two feet in front of him and did virtually nothing to dispel the darkness around him. He heard each breath he took in the quiet stillness, and the slight gritty sound his boots made as he walked on the road.

He jumped and spun to the right as the sound of a small creature darting through the underbrush broke the silence. He could only see weeds and dead leaves from the previous fall. A couple stalks of tall, dry grass quivered. He swallowed hard and turned his flashlight back to the road.

His heart was pounding and he was beginning to doubt his decision to capture evidence of Bigfoot when he came upon the portion of the road where they'd had the encounter that morning. There were strips of curving black lines where the tires had left behind their imprint when the bus had swerved and stopped, so he knew he was in the right place. Fleetingly, he thought of Mrs. Crowley and the way she'd screamed. He hoped she was all right—the shock and trauma had left her unable to even speak.

Standing completely still in the thick shroud of night, he listened intently, hoping—yet dreading—he would hear the sound of something large lurking in the surrounding woods.

Except there was only silence, and the hoot of a distant owl.

"Now all I have to do is find the trail," he whispered to himself, his voice shaking.

C'mon, don't be scared. You survived before. You'll manage now. He thought, giving himself an internal pep-talk.

He walked along the edge of the road, the same side he'd seen Bigfoot disappear from, slowly scanning the underbrush with his flashlight. It took him less than five minutes to spot where the grass had been pressed down by the creature's large feet; the blades were still flat.

"You really are big," Josh muttered and tried to see deeper into the forest, wishing the trees didn't block out so much of the wane moonlight, even though it barely helped.

"Well, here I come," he said with a sigh, stepping off the road and heading into the unknown.

After twenty minutes or so of crunching through the woods, he gave up on trying to be quiet. Even in the cool air he was sweating and breathing heavily, repeatedly tripping and falling over things he couldn't see.

He sat down on a fallen tree trunk and tried to catch his breath, seriously thinking about returning home. He sat the bag with the camera inside it beside him, and nearly jumped out of his skin when he heard the snap of a twig behind him not ten yards away. He slid off the log, grabbing the camera case, and drew it to him. He tore the bag open as fast as he could and extracted the camera before turning off his flashlight.

Another snapping twig, this one closer, sounded from the other side of the log. In one smooth motion, he stood up, turning on the camera's light and recording at the same time.

"Hey!" a young male voice yelled. "What are you doing?"

"What the—?" Josh said, lowering the camera, noticing that it wasn't Bigfoot, but a strangely dressed young man with a shotgun. "Who are you? And what's with the hat? What's with the freakin' gun?"

"My name's Elijah," he said, blinking and looking around, trying to get the light spots out of his eyes. "I'm Amish—we all dress like this. The gun is for the bear that killed our cow and scared my sister. I'm going to hunt it down and kill it, even though my father forbade me to act. He says it's against God's will, but I won't stand by and let my family be hurt! What are you doing in the woods in the middle of the night, flashing people with lights?"

"Um, okay." He didn't want to sound stupid or crazy. "I'm looking for proof that Bigfoot is real. Sorry I blinded ya, and about your sister. He attacked my school bus this morning . . . . Wait a second! What kind of cow got killed? Was it tan, sorta?"

Elijah looked at him, still blinking the light from his eyes. "Bessie was a Brown Swiss, so, ya, she was tan."

"Dude!" Josh exclaimed in shock. "Bigfoot killed and ate your cow!"

Elijah frowned and stopped rubbing his eyes. "There's no such thing as Bigfoot."

Josh dragged a hand through his hair. "Yes, there is! He attacked the bus I was on this morning and he had a cow's head with him."

"But . . . but . . . that can't be true," Elijah said. "Are you sure it wasn't a bear? We aren't supposed to have those either, but they live in most of the surrounding states, so I don't see why there wouldn't be some in Ohio, too."

"It wasn't a bear!" Josh screamed, angry now. "It was Bigfoot!"

As if on cue to prove him right, a bellowing roar sounded off to their left.

Elijah chattered something in a language Josh didn't understand and raised the shotgun to his shoulder, facing the direction of the roar. Josh did the same, except with the camera.

Leaves rustled and branches snapped as the large shadow of a hair-covered, humanoid form came charging at them, teeth bared. A loud roar that sounded like thunder shook Josh to his core.

The blast of the shotgun as Elijah pulled the trigger echoed throughout the night, overpowering everything else and deafening Josh's ears. The flare of fire from the muzzle showed him what they were up against.

Bigfoot—even hunched over in a run—was over seven feet tall, and was obscenely muscular. But what disconcerted him the most was the blood-lust in the being's eyes as it headed straight for them.

Elijah quickly pumped another shell into the chamber when he realized he'd missed with his first shot. . .but it was too late. Bigfoot was upon them. It went after Josh first, attracted and annoyed by the light on the camera.

Josh screamed as he was lifted and thrown against a tall, thick tree. After his spine broke with a sickening snap, he went silent and fell limply to the ground; the camera landed beside him, still recording.

◆　◆　◆

Elijah shot again, this time from point-blank range. The shot scattered and ripped a patch of hair from the monster's stomach, wounding it slightly. Its hand shot out and gripped him by the neck, lifting him from the ground. It took hold of his leg with the other hand and tore off the boy's head and leg.

◆　◆　◆

Bigfoot dropped the severed limbs, which landed at odd angles with the body they'd just come from, and sniffed the air, before dragging off both of the carcasses to his lair.

◆　◆　◆

After two days of searching, Josh's camera and Elijah's gun were found in the woods. The police noted there were signs of a struggle and blood was present, otherwise they had no more leads . . . until they watched the tape. After they watched the filmed carnage, a new search was organized, this one with fully-armed men. They scoured the woods in search of the monster that'd killed the young boys, but to no avail.

The tape was never released.

◆　◆　◆

Deep in a cavern in a rock formation close to Salt Fork State Park, Bigfoot gorged on the succulent, tender flesh of the boys he'd killed, biding his time until he could go out again and hunt freely, when the humans had finally given up searching for what they'd never find. With each scrape of his teeth against bone, more evidence disappeared into a beast that, in most people's rational mind, didn't exist—a hungry beast that only wanted fresh meat and would stop at nothing to get it.

SAVAGE INTENTIONS

BY

S. NYCOLE LAFF

THEY FOUND THE boy's remains draped across a bench in the park. His intestines piled in his lap, spilling down onto his ankles. One eye was missing, as was half of his nose. His fingers were still gripping the sleeve of his sister's coat, but the little girl was nowhere to be found.

A middle-aged man eyed the remains with a mixture of interest and disgust. The boy couldn't have been more than eleven or twelve, and judging by the size of the coat, the girl was closer to eight or nine. School had been out for a few hours, and his best guess was the two kids had been on their way home from school, when they were attacked.

"Stupid wild dogs," Detective Burrows said. "They were only kids! No matter how long I'm on this job, I don't never get use to seein' kids all ripped up like this."

Knowing the perps were dogs, and not humans, left him feeling even more useless. At least when the bad guy is a guy, you could hunt him down and bring him to justice. These were just wild animals, and who knew if they'd ever be caught and killed? If they cut back the department any more, they might as well give this part of the city over to the animals.

As more and more people moved out of Detroit, large parts of the city were abandoned and left to return to nature. Feral dogs grouped together in packs that became bigger and braver. This was the third attack this month, and the second little girl to go missing. Burrows figured the dogs had run her down to exhaustion, and then dragged her back to their den, which was probably in one of the many worn-down, dilapidated buildings that had become so common. In the past year, more than one hundred people had gone missing, and only four of them had been accounted for. One of those was found by vagrants in a building that they shared with a feral cat community. The cats were apparently so nice as to let the humans crash there from time to time.

Ducking under the police tape, Burrows tucked away his notebook and walked over to the officer in charge. He flicked his half-smoked cigarette to the street, grinding it out in disgust.

"Another one of those wild dog attacks. It all just disgusts me, the way this town is going to pot. First there's the gangs, which wasn't too bad, because those idiots just mostly killed each other. Then all of the businesses started to abandon ship, like the rats they are. And now this packs of wild animals driving us humans out of our own neighborhoods."

Lt. Baxter nodded. Burrows knew he'd heard it all before, there just wasn't jack-all he could do about it.

"Why don't you head home, Burrows, I've got it from here. Just have your report on my desk in the morning."

Burrows gave a grunt and a nod and headed down the street to his car.

◆ ◆ ◆

The creature called Jag-we held his prize tight to his chest, her unconscious body swinging like a rag doll with each long stride. He had to make it back to his *umbegdo* before the next sun came for the ritual to be complete. After sixteen summers, he would finally be *gebbindwa*, a full member of his *umbegdo*, and as soon as his prize began to bleed, he could take her as his mate. Until then, she would serve the other needs of his *umbegdo* in the ways of their young. Five suns ago, his older brother, Jag-du, had returned long after the sun took the sky, and was forced to devour his prize, ensuring he would never breed. Jag-we and Jag-du were the last two of their *umbegdo* to pass sixteen summers. The new ones, those with smooth coats, were many summers from their *gebbindwa*. It was sixteen summers ago the last mate of their kind passed, leaving them to hunt and gather new mates, so the *umbegdo* would live on and please the gods.

Jag-we slowed his pace as he approached the woods, many, many strides from where he captured his prize. The no-hairs would not find him here, and the moon was still young up above him. He crouched near a tree to examine his catch. Her eyes were still closed, and he worried she had left him to join the no-hair gods. As he bent forward to sniff her face and hair, he felt her breath lightly on his cheek. His eerie howl filled the woods, announcing he had returned with a suitable no-hair mate. He threw his prize over his shoulder and ran to greet his pack mates.

◆ ◆ ◆

Jag-du scowled as he heard his brother's howl. It was wrong that the younger cub should have a mate, while he wouldn't. Jag-du would never be *gebbindwa*. He would always be seen as a cub in his *umbegdo*, never able to hunt or mate. On the next moon, they would cut his cups of strength from his body, and offer them to the gods. Unless . . . Jag-du's ears twitched as the idea came to him.

With a victorious howl of his own, he loped off into the forest to claim a prize above all others.

◆　◆　◆

This time they found the body bent forward over a park bench, with her dress ripped off and bits of cloth around her ankles. To say she had been raped was an understatement. Large patches of hair had been ripped out by the roots, taking chunks of scalp with it. Blood had pooled from the four parallel grooves that were carved into each thigh, and her bare back was covered in bloody, gaping bite-marks. Her face was locked in a mask of sheer terror.

The first cop on the scene was a rookie, who was still losing his breakfast in the bushes beside the path.

Detective Burrows took a deep breath and moved forward to examine the scene. He glanced at his watch; it was way too early in the morning to deal with this crap. If he didn't know any better, he'd have thought the victim had been raped by some sort of wild animal. What kind of monster could do this to a woman? In his twenty-three years on the force, he had seen a lot of horrible things, but never anything this brutal.

Just as he was kneeling down to get a closer look at the victim's feet, his cell phone chirped. He stood up and answered it, happy for the reprieve from the grueling scene.

"Yeah, this is Burrows."

"Hey, Detective, we've been getting some weird reports coming in from the area around that crime scene."

"What kind of reports?"

"Well, um, witnesses are saying they saw a guy in some sort of ape suit running around there."

"What!? An ape suit? Listen, Reynolds, I don't have time to chase some idiot who's decided to wander around the park dressed up like an ape!"

"But, the reports . . ."

"Spit it out, Sergeant, I don't have all day."

"Well, a couple of the reports said there was a lot of blood on the, um, fur of the suit . . . and that the suit was, er . . . anatomically correct."

"Let me get this straight. You're telling me my rapist is some sort of lunatic running around in an anatomically-correct ape costume? You've got to be kidding me."

Burrows pulled the phone away from his ear and gave it an incredulous look as he hit the END button. He could barely process what the desk sergeant had told him. What kind of sick . . . . Last year the department had this big training on internet trends and crime. He'd gotten a good chuckle out of the whole discussion about some subculture called "Furries," but the presenter hadn't talked about anything even remotely like this, about guys who dressed in animal costumes and went around killing people.

Stepping away from the bench, he pulled out a fresh cigarette and lit it; he had some thinking to do. But first, he needed to call Sergeant Reynolds back and have him make sure the press didn't get a hold of this "ape man" information. He could just see the headlines now: "Bigfoot Rapist on the Loose".

Stupid furries.

◆　◆　◆

Jag-du groomed the no-hair's blood off of his deep auburn coat, savoring the taste and scent with each pass. His idea did not work as planned. At first he was unsure of how to mate with the female, and when she started howling for her pack, his blood began to rush. He had never felt such power before. With so much power, he could be *Mbugu* and above all others in his tribe. He drew each long claw across his pronounced canines, cleaning out the matted blood and flesh. Yes, he had found the source of power in her fear. Now he would gather more, and would soon be *Mbugu*.

Jag-du finished grooming and settled in to sleep the day away. He had found a very tall, no-hair hut that no longer held the no-hair stink. He took shelter in the large tree that had grown in through the window, and soon was dreaming of being a god.

◆　◆　◆

Dani twisted her wrists back and forth, but the strips of sheets wouldn't budge. Tears streamed down her face as she realized the ties were just too strong for her to move, especially in her weakened state. She wasn't sure how long she had been trapped in the stinking, burned-out building, but she knew things stopped making sense a long time ago. At first she'd thought she'd been grabbed by some freak in an ape suit. She hadn't been hooking very long, but she knew there were some real weirdoes out there. It didn't take much time for her to figure out it was something much worse, something so terrible she wished it was only a freak in an ape suit.

Her heart raced as she heard the monster's cry echoing through the abandoned building. It would be back soon. Taking a deep breath, she began to beat her head against the floor, hoping she'd knock herself out and not have to face the thing again.

◆　◆　◆

Jag-du heard the rhythmic pounding as he jogged up the stairs three or four at a time. His face twisted in rage with each step. He rushed into the tree-den just in time to see his mate collapse to the floor. A quiet growl rumbled through the den after he bent to sniff her. For the past three moons, her scent had been different; the bitter smell of fear was still there, but she now smelled of something sweet. It was like the mating smell, but not as . . . fire-making.

Jag-du groomed his sleeping mate, savoring the hot taste of her blood. As she slept, he watched her carefully. It seemed her middle was growing bigger. Soon he would have a smooth-coat cub to bring back to his *umbegdo*, and then he would be *gebbindwa*, and his power would destroy all who did not come to his side. It had been four moons since he found his mate, each of the suns spent gathering food for the two of them. On each brightest moon, he gathered more power from those who would never be his mate.

◆　◆　◆

Detective Burrows stared at the newspaper as he took a long drag off his cigarette. BIGFOOT SERIAL KILLER RAPIST STRIKES AGAIN! the headlines declared. He'd been able to keep the story out of the papers for a few weeks, but after the third body turned up, all hell broke loose. Of course, he didn't think "furry serial killer rapist" sounded much better.

Exhaling, then taking a last swig of his coffee, Burrows stubbed out his cigarette and headed outside to his car. He couldn't believe they didn't even have a hint of a suspect yet. Seven months of investigation and nothing. Each scene was more gruesome than the last, and the only description they could get of the perp was of some guy in an anatomically-correct ginger ape costume, with long, sharp claws and the scariest mask anyone had ever seen. Officers had combed every costume shop, tracking down anyone who had rented an ape costume in the last year, but nothing came of it. Some of the tracks left at the crime scenes had been freakishly large, so he knew they were looking for a big guy, probably six-five or six-six and at least three hundred and fifty pounds. None of the shops they contacted even had costumes that size, and sure enough, when they'd got in touch with all of the renters and buyers, none of them were over six-two.

Sliding behind the wheel, Burrows thought back to the last scene. It had been the worst yet. It seemed the killer was no longer satisfied just to rape and mutilate his victims, but now he was stealing their hearts right out of their chests. Burrows could only think of a few reasons for someone to do that, and none of them were particularly good. His biggest fear was that his Bigfoot serial killer rapist was now also a cannibal. Wouldn't the press just go to town with that little piece of information. This crap was giving him a headache. Popping the car into drive, he headed back to the station to look over the evidence again for anything he might have missed. Maybe if he stared at it all long enough, the answer would appear.

Burrows gave a sardonic snort. Yeah, and maybe the tooth fairy was real, and his perp really was an honest-to-God Sasquatch. Yeah, this crap was really messed up.

◆　◆　◆

A burnt-orange sunset filled the room as Dani absently chewed on the raw meat the creature fed her. In the back of her mind, she noticed it was a lot chewier than what he usually offered. None of it was really real anymore. She knew the truth—she had died the night the creature attacked her and was now in Hell. Momma had always told her she was going to Hell for all of the bad things she had done, and wow, lookie here, her momma was right. She could see the light of the hellfire that flickered around the building. *You'd think with all that fire, I wouldn't have to eat raw meat!* Dani chuckled like a lunatic as she sucked down the rest of the meat. The laughter triggered another round of kicking from the creature inside of her. Her haunted eyes watched with disinterest as her belly rippled with each impact. Yeah, this must be Hell. If it wasn't, she'd be dead by now. The baby had already reduced her to skin and bones, and it felt like it was going to rip her open any minute. She really wished it would, because then maybe it would all be over. But then again, if this was Hell, it would probably all just reset and start again.

Her dinner finished, Dani slid to the floor and started to drift off again.

Soon, the searing pain in her stomach brought her wide awake. More awake than she'd been in months. Hearing her cries, the creature appeared beside her, his coat a reddish-gold in the light of the fire behind him. He stared at her belly. She was afraid to look. It felt like hundreds of snakes were slithering around inside of her. She shuddered with revulsion as the movement and pain intensified. Dani struggled to sit up and immediately she began to vomit, her body convulsing with each retch. Once the heaving stopped, she dragged her arm across her face and her eyes were drawn to the movement inside of her: the skin of her belly stretched thin as the thing inside her pressed its hands—paws—against the walls of her womb. Struck with horror, she couldn't look away. She watched in fascination as the elasticity of her skin was tested again and again by limbs far larger than they should be. Her upper body started to slide back to the floor just as four razor-sharp claws ripped through the flesh on either side of her abdomen. Dani screamed.

"What is happening to me? What did you do to me? It's tearing me apart!"

The creature reached down and placed his huge hands on either side of her head. With a quick twist, the screaming was over.

◆　◆　◆

As the smooth-haired cub—now called Wag-du—finally worked his way out of the bloody, shredded ruins of his mate's body, Jag-du's victory howl brought the wild city to silence. Jag-du showed his son how to tear off pieces of flesh and eat them. The newborn first sucked the blood off of each piece, and then shredded it with his small, sharp teeth. Father and son feasted, and soon there was nothing recognizable left of what had been his mate. Jag-du groomed his cub to sleep, and then slowly groomed himself as he prepared for his triumphant return. He would kill his brother and rule his *umbegdo*.

◆ ◆ ◆

An eerie howl pierced the night and Detective Burrows hoped he would live to regret not calling in for back up. Tips had been coming in for weeks and he had been able to narrow down the building where the perp was living. When four more reports came in from that general area, he grabbed his coat and keys and hopped into the car. It wasn't until he got to the building that he realized he'd left his cell phone sitting in the top drawer of his desk.

"Well, there's nothing I can do about it now." His whisper seemed to boom in the silence of the jungle around him. Burrows shuddered. With his gun in one hand and his flashlight in the other, he entered the overgrown building.

Shining the light, he cautiously took in the room around him. Crumbling walls were crawling with vines and there were piles of feces and garbage everywhere. The reek took his breath away and it was all he could do not to puke right there. He tucked the gun into his waistband and grabbed a dirty, white handkerchief out of his back pocket. Holding the flashlight in his mouth, he tied the piece of cloth around the back of his head so it covered his nose and mouth. He pocketed the flashlight, adjusted the handkerchief, and took an experimental breath. Not too bad. He grabbed his light and his gun, and headed for the stairs.

As he approached the top floor of the building, Burrows heard an odd cry, like a cross between a mewling baby and some sort of animal grunting. Aiming the flashlight at the floor, he crept toward the sound. The closer he got, the worse it smelled around him. But the smell had changed. It was sweeter now and more pungent. It reminded him of his sister's sugar gliders.

He saw the flicker of firelight as he approached the last doorway on the top floor. Both the stink and the sounds seemed to be coming from that direction. Clicking it off and pocketing his light, he quietly inched across the threshold. He noticed what looked like his ape-suited killer rapist cradling a small child. The dim firelight didn't help him make sense of what he was seeing. If he didn't know better, he'd think he was looking at a real-life Bigfoot with some sort of hybrid kid. Suddenly he remembered reading about a circus freak, whose body and face were covered in hair. Wasn't that condition genetic? He was pretty sure it was. He couldn't believe he hadn't thought of it sooner. He crept a few feet closer and aimed his gun at the guy. He didn't want to fire and accidentally hit the kid.

"Set the kid down and put your hands up!" Decades of experience gave his voice more confidence than he felt.

The perp's head snapped up at the sound. Burrows gasped. The creature's face was horribly deformed—it looked like some sort of gorilla mask, with amber, human eyes. Dropping the kid, the creature lunged at him. Reacting, Burrows fired. He emptied his clip into the thing, but it just kept coming. His mouth was still forming a scream when the creature knocked his head off of his body.

◆ ◆ ◆

Jag-du growled in rage as he threw the no-hair's head against the brick wall, where it burst into several pieces. Kneeling down, Jag-du picked up the no-hair's brain, ripped it to chunks, and then hurled the pieces around the room.

He grabbed his son off the floor and positioned the cub on his back. The cub instinctively dug his fingers into his father's coat and held on as his father ran for the stairs.

They ran for many strides in the trees before the pain overtook Jag-du. As the sun took to the sky, he saw many oozing holes in his coat, each leaking blood. Wag-du dropped down from his father's back and crawled over to groom the blood from Jag-du's coat. Jag-du cradled his son to his chest, mewling softly. The mewling ended as the sun rose to its highest point.

Still suckling from his dead father's wounds, Wag-du whimpered and began to feed.

◆ ◆ ◆

The sleeping child awoke to the sounds of yips and growls all around him in the darkness; a pack of wolves had circled him and his dead father. Snarling and snapping, the wolves took turns lunging forward and falling back. Hunger and the scent of blood made them braver with each pass until finally one sunk its teeth into the dead creature's ankle and yanked it backwards. The rest of the pack immediately fell upon the body, ripping and tearing it to shreds as the confused child watched. The corpse was quickly devoured, and the wolves circled the child once more, growling and licking at their blood-stained muzzles. Pain-filled shrieks filled the air as the wolves ripped the child's limbs from his body. Soon, the woods fell abruptly silent except for the wet sounds of the pack devouring its prey.

SHADES OF SASQUATCH

BY

A.M. BURNS

THE BELL ON the door lightly jingled as Steve Marsden followed his mother into the Pine Valley Lodge Gallery. It was the third gallery-boutique they had visited since setting out a couple of hours before. Like the other two, log furniture and carved bears dominated the inventory. His mother had already bought a log-framed couch, two log beds, several log benches, and a set of carved bears for the new cabin.

At least this store had interesting pictures on the wall, Steve thought, as his mother engaged the sales clerk.

Steve wandered over and looked at a large painting of running wolves framed with heavy logs. The painting felt strangely powerful. It looked like the wolves could come running out of it at any second.

The door jingled again. Steve turned and his stepbrother Jamie slumped in.

"So this is where you guys ran off to." Jamie panted from the long walk up the hill from the last store. Sweat dripped from his flattened, black hair down his oily, acne-covered forehead.

"Yeah, Mom saw the sign and had to check it out."

"I wonder if Dad knows she's spending all his money up here?" Jamie said.

On the one hand Steve could understand watching out for your birth parents' interest, but Jamie always complained about every penny Steve's mom spent. "He said she could do what she needed to do to make the place livable."

A red lampshade caught Steve's eye. He walked away from Jamie before his stepbrother could say anything else. A pattern of green trees encircled the shade. It looked like it might be one of those lampshades that had something hidden in the image. He reached over the bark-covered log base, and pulled the little gold chain. A soft light illuminated the shade, and suddenly large furry forms appeared amongst the trees. It looked like the silhouette on a sign one of their neighbors marked the driveway to his cabin with. Sasquatch was huge right now.

"Mom, look at this," Steve called across the nearly vacant store.

"Steven!" She then said something softly to the clerk before storming over. "Steven, you should know better than to shout across a store." Sometimes she treated him like he was ten instead of eighteen.

"Sorry," he said softly, "but I wanted you to see this cool lampshade." He gestured to the red shade. "It would look great on my nightstand."

"That's just tacky," she said with a frown.

"It will be in my room."

"Well . . ."

"We could get one of those for Jamie." He pointed to the similar shades with wolves and bears on them that had seemed to catch Jamie's eye judging by the way he intently peered at it.

"At least they would match," his mother said with a defeated sigh. She went over to find out which one Jamie wanted.

Steve turned the light off and on a couple of times, watching the shadow of Bigfoot appear and disappear.

◆　　◆　　◆

Two days later all the furniture began arriving, and his mother seemed to be everywhere at once. She had Steve and Jamie carry all the old furniture out onto the side of the driveway. She directed the delivery men where to put everything.

Jamie complained the whole time. "My mother never did things like this. The stuff Dad put up here was always fine with her. She *never* came up here."

"I wish it was winter so we could go skiing," Steve said after Jamie had dropped his end of the couch going down the steps.

"Careful with that or Goodwill won't take it!" his mother yelled from behind them, her arms full of cushions.

It amazed Steve the workmen never complained as his mother had them move things around several times before she was satisfied with the look of each room.

The two full-sized beds with a matching chest of drawers and nightstands for the downstairs bedroom went in with the least amount of fuss. The lamps with their slightly different shades looked exactly the way Steve thought they would.

"You know," his mother said softly as he turned on the lamp for the first time, "the lady at the store said that was one of a kind. She'd never seen the artist make a red one before. And that is the last Bigfoot lamp she had, says they sell out fast, all except that one. Say she's had it for years. With everything else we bought, she just gave it to me." His mother ruffled his blond hair. "Enjoy it."

◆　◆　◆

The light of the full moon blazed through the bare window as Steve and Jamie came into the bedroom. It hung low enough in the sky that the porch didn't block it.

"Why is it so bright?" Jamie whined as he turned on the light next to his bed. Wolves appeared from behind the trees on the lampshade. He didn't seem to notice.

"I guess the moon is brighter out here in the mountains than it is back home in Denver," Steve said absentmindedly while staring at the Bigfoot that appeared when he turned on his lamp. The red glow from the shade overpowered the moonlight and gave everything on his side of the room a soft rose hue.

Somewhere in the forest outside the cabin, muffled by the closed window, a coyote yipped.

"What was that?" Jamie asked, dropping his iPad on the unmade bed.

"Probably just a coyote," Steve replied, moving a few things so he could start making his bed.

"Is it close?" Jamie's voice shook slightly.

"It's probably just hunting rabbits or mice or something. Trust me, you're a bit more than it would want to take on." Steve suppressed a laugh. Even at eighteen, Jamie was already nearly three hundred pounds, and he doubted there was much muscle on his short frame.

"I never liked coming up here with Dad. Mom didn't either." Jamie sat down on the bed without moving any of the linens or boxes piled there.

"I think it's cool up here," Steve said, tucking the stiff sheet around the new mattress. He and his mom had spent the previous day hiking in the area around the cabin while Jamie stayed in and played games on his iPad.

A couple minutes later they heard a yelp; sounded like a dog getting hurt.

"I hope someone scared off that coyote," Jamie said, leaning back against the pillows and putting his feet on one of the boxes.

Steve sighed. He finished making the bed, then stared out the window for a minute. He thought he saw some movement in the trees just down the hill from the cabin, but decided it was probably just the coyote. He decided not to tell Jamie about it. He didn't want his stepbrother staying up all night scared. He turned from the window, and turned off his light as he crawled into his bed. "Night, Jamie."

"Night," was all Jamie could spare from his game.

◆　◆　◆

A loud scream tore Steve from his sleep. "What?" He rubbed at his eyes.

Jamie sat on his bed, his knees pulled up to his prominent belly, and pointed to the window. "Eyes," he stammered, his own wide in the faint light of the iPad in his hand.

Steve looked at the window. He couldn't see any eyes there. "I guess you scared it off."

"Go look," Jamie demanded in a hard whisper.

"As if," Steve settled himself back on his pillow.

"Go look or I'll go get your mom and have her look. Maybe the coyote will eat her."

Steve rolled over and pulled the chain on his lamp. The soft red glow lit the room closer to the window. "I'll go look. Do you remember where Mom put the flashlights?"

"No, I don't remember where your mother put the flashlights."

"Well, come on then, let's go find a flashlight and take a look around outside." Steve ran a hand through his short blond hair, trying to flatten it down. Then decided it really didn't matter. He was unlikely to meet anyone who would care if his hair was standing up or not.

"I'm not going out there."

"If you don't come, I'm not going. This is your thing not mine. I can let everyone know you're afraid of the woods." Steve stopped pulling on his hikers and glared.

"Fine, but you go first."

"Fine."

They found the flashlights in a drawer next to the back door. Steve handed one to Jamie and took one for himself.

The trees grew thick at the back of the cabin, but a small trail led around toward the front of the house. Steve led the way. Nothing made a sound as they walked around the cabin, following the trail that would lead them past their window.

The soft red glow from Steve's lamp looked like blood on the leaves of the aspen tree closest to the house. Without the moonlight the forest lay dark and foreboding. His mind raced at what might be out there waiting for them. He imagined crafty coyotes, bold bears, marauding mountain lions, and even stealthy Sasquatches waiting to pounce and carry them away.

"What was that?" Jamie said, and pointed off to the left with his flashlight.

Steve swept the area with his light. All he saw was a lot of last year's leaves, and a couple of fallen limbs. "Can't see anything."

"Well, I know I heard something."

"Let's keep looking." Steve started back toward the glow from their window.

A couple more steps and they stood just outside their window. Steve moved his light over the area, looking for anything out of the ordinary. Near the tree some of the leaves looked flatter than the leaves around them, like something had stood there. He stepped off the path, going to get a closer look.

"Where are you going?" Jamie's voice held an edge of panic.

"Just want to look at the base of this tree."

"Why?"

He ignored the question.

Around the aspen, the leaves did indeed look squished. Something had walked on them, but he wondered how long ago. He looked up. His head barely came up to Jamie's knees due to the incline of the hill. If something had stood there and looked into their window it had to be taller than his six-foot-two. It must have been at least eight feet tall. He passed the light up and down the tree. He couldn't see anything out of the ordinary aside from the flattened leaves at the bottom.

"Hey, do you smell something?" Jamie called down louder than he needed to.

Steve took a deep breath. A heavy musky smell, skunk-like, assaulted his nose. "Yeah, but I think it is just a skunk."

"There are skunks up here?" Jamie sounded like a girl.

"I don't know. I guess if we're smelling one, then there are skunks up here."

He flashed the light on the side of the incline back to the trail around the house so he could see his footing. There in the light was part of a foot print. Long and narrow, the print was missing the front part of the foot. He couldn't tell exactly how big the print should have been. He placed his own foot in its size-twelve hikers next to the print. Even as a partial, it eclipsed his foot. He stared at it for a second. It reminded him of cast of Bigfoot prints he'd seen on TV. Either that or an enormous gorilla.

"I'm going back inside." Jamie headed toward the backdoor.

"I'm going to look around a bit more," Steve replied, scanning the ground for more footprints. "You might want to go ahead and let Mom know what's going on."

"Okay."

Steve scratched his chin as his flashlight passed over the ground. He liked the feel of the growing stubble on his skin and wondered if the girls would like it.

The skunk smell grew stronger.

He couldn't tell where the wind came from. He glanced up, and saw Jamie's light disappearing around the corner of the cabin. At least he wouldn't have to listen to his stepbrother's whining for a few minutes.

Jamie screamed.

Steve climbed the slight incline back to the trail in two steps. His long strong legs carried him around the corner in a couple of seconds.

He ducked as something flew toward him.

The object bounced off the side of the cabin with a heavy thud, then rolled to stop at his feet.

In the beam of his flashlight, Jamie's empty brown eyes stared up at him.

Steve took a couple of steps backward, heart racing..

His stomach lurched.

A deep, menacing growl came from near the back door.

"Boys, what's going on?" Steve heard his mother call from somewhere in the cabin.

He pointed his light toward the growl.

A pair of huge hairy hands held Jamie's headless body aloft. The creature must have stood at least seven and a half, maybe eight feet tall. Long shaggy hair covered it. It turned its head as Steve's light passed over its face. A second later, the creature hurled Jamie's body at him.

Steve ducked around the corner again and Jamie's body thumped against a tree with a wet mushy thud.

Steve looked frantically for something, anything, he could defend himself with. He remembered that Jamie's dad had a shotgun standing near the backdoor of the cabin, but that was inside. Maybe he could get around front before the creature caught him?

He raced toward the front door.

Behind him an unearthly scream sent shivers up and down his spine.

Steve leapt onto the wooden porch that ran around half of the house, then turned the front corner of the cabin. He heard heavy steps running on the path behind him. The skunk smell grew stronger. He grabbed the doorknob on the front door.

It was locked.

Heavy running footsteps shook the boards beneath his feet as the thing jumped to the porch without using the three steps leading to it.

Steve spotted the open living room window. Dropping the flashlight, he hurled himself through. The landing on the hardwood floor knocked the wind out of him for a second.

"Boys?" He heard his mother open the backdoor.

"Mom, don't go out there!" Steve screamed. He scrambled to his feet as the first furry fist landed on the front door.

He saw the light on in the kitchen, and raced through the cabin toward it.

The pounding on the door became more intense.

"Steven, what's going on?" She stood there in her robe, her hands on her hips and a demanding glare on her face.

"There's something out there," Steve replied in heavy gasp. "Jamie saw it first. We went to see what it was. I think it might be a Bigfoot."

The front door crashed under the onslaught from outside.

His mother paled, and her nearly alabaster skin looked even more deathly.

"Where's the shotgun?" he asked, trying to look around his mother toward the back door.

Heavy footsteps echoed off the hardwood floor of the living room.

"Why? Do you think a shotgun will help? When did you learn to shoot?" She sounded sleepy and confused.

"Last summer, at camp, and It can't hurt. That thing already killed Jamie!" Steve spotted the gun, and dashed toward it.

"What killed Jamie?" she demanded as the creature came through the doorway. Her eyes widened in horror at the sight.

In the glare of the kitchen light the thing looked more terrifying than it had by flashlight. It filled the doorway, having to stoop a bit to fit through. The long hair was a dull brown. The stench filled the room before the creature did. Steve gagged and heard his mother gurgle a soft scream.

He threw the backdoor open as he snatched up the shotgun. "Mom, get out!"

Luckily she was closer to the door than the creature. She ran toward Steve as he brought the gun up to his shoulder. He pulled the trigger. The hammer merely clicked. He stared at the shotgun in disbelief. "Where are the shells?"

She screamed.

He turned and dropped the gun. His mother stood staring at Jamie's headless body up against the tree.

The creature pushed through the doorway and into the small kitchen.

Steve jumped out of the back door and pulled it closed behind him.

"I told you Jamie was dead! We need to get out of here!" He ran toward her.

Her long blonde hair hid the tears rolling down her cheeks. "Jamie. No . . . . What am I going to tell James?" She fell to her knees next to the body of her stepson.

Pounding began again. The creature was trying to get out of the backdoor.

"We'll tell him the truth," Steve said, pulling her up by the shoulders. He really didn't care what they told his stepfather at this point. He wanted to get out of there. "Where are the car keys?" He pushed her toward the front driveway where their new Range Rover sat.

"In my purse by the bed." She sounded more dazed than scared.

Steve heard the glass in the door shatter.

"Okay, maybe I can get to my set." He had left his set on his nightstand, but it would be easier to get into the main level of the house than the loft. "You get to the car. Then lock the doors. I'll be there as fast as I can."

"Where are you going?" His mother sounded like she was about to argue with him.

"To get my keys. I'm going through this window." They had reached the window where the red light glowed.

Steve heard the backdoor splinter. "Mom, go! I'll be right there." He shoved her toward the front of the cabin. He kicked the window with all his might. The window cracked. A second kick went through, sending glass flying into the room.

The window sill was low enough that he could duck through it.

Glass crunched under foot as he walked toward the nightstand. The silhouettes on the lampshade seemed more sinister now, almost alive. He knew it was all in his head but he couldn't shake the feeling. He had a strange impulse to turn it off, but he wanted the light. His keys glistened in the pale light under the lamp. He grabbed them then looked back toward the window in time to see the hairy form run past. Like the leaves of the aspen tree the furry form was tainted red in the light of the shade. Then it was gone.

Steve paused a second, wondering where the shotgun shells might be. He could go back to the kitchen and get the gun, but where would Mom or James have put the shells?

His mother screamed from the front of the house.

He dashed out of the room and down the short hall toward the living room. The remains of the front door lay splintered across the new log-framed couch that had been delivered only hours before. Steve ran for the opening where the door had been.

He heard the monster's high-pitched call again.

Standing on the porch, he tried to see his mother in the dark of the night. He spotted his flashlight, still on, laying near the front window. He had completely forgotten he had dropped it there. He snatched it up and swept the area in front of the cabin.

Right in front of the Range Rover, the creature had hold of his mother. She hung limply in his grasp and he couldn't tell if she was alive or not.

"Let her go!" he shouted, bringing the flashlight around to shine in the thing's eyes.

The creature dropped her and tried to shield its eyes from the light.

Legs rubbery, panic setting in, Steve tried to think of what to do. He wanted to get his mother away from the thing, but he had seen what it had done to Jamie. He wished the shotgun had been loaded, or that he had a baseball bat or something.

Then he spotted the pile of boxes that the furniture guys had left behind. He remembered that some of the boxes had wooden supports in them. It might not be a baseball bat, but he might be able to at least make an impression on the creature.

Starting toward the pile, he kept the light on the beast. It backed away a couple of steps then knelt down in the driveway.

Its hand moved faster than Steve could follow, and the barrage of river stones hit him hard.

One managed to find the flashlight. The impact knocked it out of his hand. It went out went it hit the ground. One of the other stones connected with his temple. His head swam, and he tried to find the flashlight again on the ground.

Before he could straighten up, Steve felt a huge hand on his shoulder, even as his fingers curled around the handle of the flashlight. He swung it up as hard as he could. A satisfying *umph* came from above him as the flashlight connected with the creature's delicate parts, and it bent over.

Rocks hurt his knees as Steve scrambled to get out of reach of the creature. The beast recovered quickly and grabbed him by the ankle.

He gagged as he swung the flashlight again while the monster pulled him up from the ground. He connected with a hairy shin and it didn't seem to care. He tried again, slamming the flashlight's hard casing against the beast's thigh. It was like hitting a rock. He tried again for the groin, but the creature swung him and he missed completely.

Then he was airborne.

His back connected with the front grill of the Range Rover. He heard metal break, and felt something in his back shatter. Body suddenly going numb, Steve dropped face first onto the hard river stone driveway. Blood oozed from his nose.

The reek of the creature engulfed him.

He felt a fleeting pressure as an enormous foot connected with the back of his head.

◆　◆　◆

The sun peeks over the nearest mountain and a pair of hairy hands hold up a red lampshade with trees painted on it. The hands tilt the lampshade so the silhouette that looks surprisingly like the owner of the hands appears. Moments later in a shallow cave, the hands place the lampshade on a rocky ledge alongside four others, each of different color.

A high-pitch cry of triumph fills the quiet morning.

EXILED

BY

GREG MITCHELL

DRY LEAVES CRUNCHED beneath his boots as Pete Foster pressed deeper into the woods.

"Dude, we're lost," Zack Stephens groaned beside him.

"Shut up, I know where I'm going."

Thirteen-year-old Pete had spent most of his young life in these Arkansas woods. His father had brought him hunting out here every autumn since he'd been able to hold a .22. These sticks were a second home to him and he resented Zack questioning his guidance.

Frustrated or bored, Zack hacked at some nearby branches with a machete. Having just discovered *Rambo* via his dad's old VHS tapes, he now fancied himself a beleaguered Vietnam vet with some sixth jungle sense. The boy swung the machete once more, tearing down a tangle of hanging twigs.

"Cut it out," Pete hissed. "You're going to scare it away."

"If it's even *out* here."

"It" in this case, was Bigfoot.

There'd been a few possible sightings over the last couple weeks, and even though authorities deemed it a hoax or some other animal, boyhood curiosity finally got the best of Pete and his friend-slash-rival Zack. They dared each other for days to investigate the story themselves. Tonight— Friday—Pete was spending the night with Zack so, after much bluster, they decided to sneak out of the Stephens' country house once Zack's parents went to bed.

Now the two boys trudged through the thick, dark woods out back, decked out in their hunting camo and armed with Pete's flashlight and Zack's machete, hoping to see Bigfoot in the hairy flesh.

"This is stupid." Zack snarled.

"It was *your* idea to come out here."

"I'm bored. Let's go back to the house and see if we can get the scrambled channels."

A rustle in the bushes up ahead. Pete froze, shining his light into the forest. "Wait," he whispered. "You hear that?"

A crack. Something heavy hitting the soft earth.

"Turn off the light," Zack snapped. "Quick."

Pete obeyed, his heart thumping hard in his chest. The boys faced each other, wide-eyed. Pete broke the eerie silence, "Should we . . . ?"

"You go first."

"You've got the machete, dude."

"You've got the light. Stop being a wuss."

Pete frowned and soundlessly inched forward, recalling his father's teachings on tracking deer. Even Zack was silent, gripping his machete close to his chest with both hands.

The two of them ascended a small knob and spotted a dark lump down below. Something was on the ground, twitching in the dried leaves. There were other sounds, too. Something crunching, and wet, slurping noises. A swallow.

"Dude . . ." Zack breathed.

The moonlight did little to expose the mystery and Pete shut his eyes tight, preparing to make his move.

"Go for it," Zack whispered, excited.

Pete held his breath, aimed the flashlight, and flicked it on.

A deer lay on the ground, dead or dying, one leg jerking in death throes. Its throat was ripped out, its muscles, skin, and tendons strewn like Christmas wrapping paper. Hunkered over the dead thing was a hairy giant, resembling a man, but too ape-like to be considered wholly human. Reddish-orange fur covered its entire body, and blood and gore streaked down its mouth and beard.

Momentarily blinded by the light, the beast—the Bigfoot—shielded its eyes and growled.

"Dude!" Zack screamed.

The boy took off running in the opposite direction, but Pete's legs would not move. Instead, he dumbly aimed his flashlight, as if frozen in time, while the Bigfoot stood, slapping away at the light's beam and gnashing its teeth.

"Pete!" Zack cried from somewhere deep in the forest. "Run, man!"

Pete did not. The Bigfoot stamped closer and Pete wet himself. The boy shut his eyes, knowing his death was imminent, but too afraid to face it. He thought of his parents and what they would say when they found out. A moment passed and Pete felt no pain. He cracked one eye open, but saw only the mangled deer.

The Bigfoot had gone.

Elated now, Pete turned tail and barreled through the forest, a smile stuck on his young face. "Zack!" he hollered. The light bobbed in front of him as he scanned the darkness. "Where'd you go? Hey, butt-wipe—"

He froze. The flashlight's beam caught a huddled mess on the forest floor, gleaming red and wearing Zack's clothes.

"Zack?"

A snarl and a black shape filled Pete's view. Dark hair and something like metal shining in moonlight was the last thing the boy saw.

◆ ◆ ◆

The semi's horn tooted and, with a hiss, it picked up speed and drove off down the sunlit highway. Dusty Rose dropped his large backpack to the asphalt and waved, appreciative. His legs felt less like Jell-O now, and he thought he could take up the walk for another couple hours before he'd have to hitch again. Of course, he was thankful for a ride anytime, but knew most folks these days weren't keen on picking up strangers on lonely country roads.

Lush trees provided shade from the afternoon sun, and the spring cool was at once comfortable and exhilarating. He took off his blue flannel over shirt and tied it around his waist, then hefted his backpack and resumed his walk east. He'd hoped to cross Arkansas today, but it seemed Fate had other things in mind. It'd be dark soon and he'd have to find a place to hole up for the night—either that or spend another night shivering under the stars.

His scuffed hiking boots kicked the gravel on the road's shoulder. Not far up the highway he spotted a roadhouse, the five o'clock customers arriving in pickups.

Dusty pressed onward.

◆ ◆ ◆

Dusty approached the roadhouse amidst the bustle of the early evening customers, looking to get started on their Saturday night. Venturing inside, he was met by raucous laughter, clinking glasses, and a jukebox in the corner playing country music. At least, he thought it was country music. It was hard to tell these days. He remembered Kenny Rogers and Hank Williams, Jr., but he was never much of a country fan really, preferring the likes of Ratt, Dokken, and Poison.

Those were good tunes. Good times, too. Concerts, parties, women, bikes, and booze. Funny how quickly good things turned bad. A few stints in prison for drug charges and auto theft later, he was a hard fifty-three—an old man now, displaced in time. An exile from another era, completely obsolete in this new age of iPods and phones that could fit in your pocket and play movies.

He shuffled up to the counter, mindful of the stares he attracted. A company of college kids in the corner couldn't take their eyes off him. Whether it was the long, bleached-blonde hair, his sun-kissed muscled arms, or his faded tattoos, young punks always found him amusing.

Dusty made his way toward the bar, trying to ignore the pointing and snickering.

"What can I get ya?" the bartender asked.

Dusty kept his head up. "Used to tend a bit back in the day. Don't suppose you're hiring?" Though he had his eye on working the boats down the Mississippi, he was prepared to settle anywhere that offered a paycheck. At least, for a while. He'd given up having a place of his own, planting roots. That wasn't for him. Not anymore.

"Sorry, pal." The bartender shook his head. "Economy's tough."

Dusty sighed with a grin. "You don't gotta tell me. I'll take a beer then."

The bartender disappeared for a second and returned with a brown bottle. Dusty paid, then took his drink over to the jukebox. He shuffled through the songs and settled on Saigon Kick's "Love is on the Way." He popped in a couple quarters—his change from the drink—and took a stool at the counter.

The chortles from the young guys were unavoidable now. At last, one of them braved, "Hey, man. 1988 just called. It wants its mullet back."

Laughter exploded from their table, but Dusty just offered a defeated smirk before taking a drink. He had been young like that, smug and invincible. Heck, if someone had talked to him like that when he was a younger man, he would have turned his face into hamburger meat. But that was a long time ago. He didn't have the strength in him now. Besides, they weren't worth the effort. Best to just finish his beer and hit the road.

Gotta keep moving, he told himself, as though some proverbial pot of gold waited for him. But there was no rainbow. No gold.

No end in sight.

The doors opened and a deputy sauntered in, his face pale and sweaty. He undid the top buttons of his uniform and near-staggered to the bar.

"Evening, Joel," the bartender said. "Usual?"

"Make it a double," Deputy Joel heaved, out of breath.

Bartender paused. "You all right?"

Joel shook his head as the bartender popped the top off a bottle. The off-duty deputy grabbed the drink. "Just found the Foster boy."

"Pete? Y'know, I haven't seen his dad tonight. He usually stops by—"

"Not tonight," the deputy said. Drank. "The boy's dead. Zack Stephens, too."

Dusty sat up. The bartender leaned on the counter, aghast. "How's that?"

"They went missing last night. We just found 'em out in the woods. All . . . all tore up. Like an animal got hold of 'em."

The bartender was quiet for a long time while the deputy guzzled. "What d'you think did it? I've heard of bobcats out here—"

"Don't know. I ain't never seen . . . I won't forget it, I'll tell ya that."

The bartender fetched a second bottle for the deputy.

Dusty nursed his own beer. Kept to himself.

"You don't think," the bartender began, hushed.

The deputy leveled a dark look. "I don't even want to think it."

"Maybe it's true. Maybe . . ."

Dusty leaned in, his curiosity pulling him closer. "What?" He surprised himself by asking out loud.

The two men balked at him, caught in their private conversation.

Dusty waved them off. "Nah, I'm sorry. None of my business."

He finished his beer and left the counter, hoisting his backpack over his broad shoulders. "Thanks for the beer," he said with a grin, headed for the door.

"Be careful," the bartender called. "Woods aren't safe at night."

"I'll manage. Y'all have a good night."

◆ ◆ ◆

If people weren't too friendly toward hitchhikers during the day, they sure weren't going to pick them up after dark. Dusty walked a couple hours before his knees began to stiffen. His joints hurt and he cursed his age.

He left the road behind, pushing through the brush into the forest while there was enough light left to set up camp. He came across a clearing and unfurled the sleeping bag tied to the top of his cumbersome backpack. His stomach grumbled and he wondered why he hadn't had the good sense to buy food with the last of his money instead of that blasted beer. Still, he had the last of a pack of jerky he'd rationed over the week that would have to do for supper. Slipping out of his boots, he unzipped the sleeping bag and slid inside. He didn't feel tired, but the sooner he went to sleep, the sooner morning would come and he could be on his way.

Ready to turn in for the night, he lit a cigarette—its twin the last in the pack—and relished it. In the fading light of dusk, Dusty removed the tattered photo he kept tucked in his billfold. He stared at himself—two decades younger—with that smug, invincible look on his face. In his arms, a tiny baby boy. His son.

He puffed on the smoke, the embers from the coffin nail illuminating his past self's pride-filled grin. And he *had* been proud that day. He and Vanessa hadn't agreed on a single thing in the seven years they were on and off, but they agreed on that boy. They loved him with all their strength.

Then Dusty got busted for "possession with intent to sell" and landed in prison.

He hadn't seen the boy since he was eight. Now that baby in the photo was twenty. A man of his own. As for Vanessa . . . she died a week ago. Cancer. Hearing she'd passed brought back a lot of conflicted emotions. He remembered the crazy times they had: partying, cruising town, loving. Then there was the fighting: the shouting and the cursing and smashing furniture. It was always love or hate with them, sometimes both. But always passionate. They broke up with as much fire as they *made* up. It seemed unfair he'd not been there in her final moments. He wondered if she thought of him and if she missed him.

And he thought of the boy. Back in California, dealing with his mom's death.

Vanessa settled down years ago. Dusty had only met her husband once, but he seemed like a decent guy. It was him, Mark, who called last week to tell him the news. How he even *found* him was a miracle and only further proof that the man was honorable to go to all that trouble. It was also Mark who told Dusty the boy needed him now. Dusty didn't know how that could be possible. Didn't know what he could possibly offer his son.

He won't want to see me, Dusty thought, touching the photo of that small baby. So tiny and fragile. He used to toss the boy in the air when he was little. Smile as he giggled, then catch him and cover him in kisses. He'd made so many silent promises back then, to stick around unlike *his* old man. He was going to be there and show the boy how to walk like a man, how to defend himself, how to hold his own.

Crazy how a bag of white powder could have made him break all those promises to his only son.

Dusty had been drug-free now for over a decade, but the shame never left. He did his best to eke out a decent living, keep his head straight, stay away from his old "friends," and stay out of trouble. But for what? What did any of it matter without the boy?

I could go back, he knew. He could turn himself around and hitch all the way back to California. Show up on the boy's doorstep and announce he was ready to be a father after all this time.

No. Just like he told Mark on the phone, the boy was better off without him.

A bestial snort, somewhere in the dark, interrupted his thoughts. On alert, he tucked his boy's picture into his shirt pocket and sat up. Seemed he had company. He was no stranger to sleeping in the woods and was well-versed in fending off occasional wildlife. Dusty reached for his Zippo and flicked it to life. Carefully, he climbed out of his sleeping bag and toed on his boots, keeping the small flickering flame before him. It did little to dispel the surrounding gloom, but he detected no shapes. Perhaps he was just being jumpy, a by-product of the bartender's ominous warning.

He thought to ask "Who's there?" but that's what stupid people did in horror movies and Dusty was neither stupid nor in a horror movie. Instead, he reached into his pack and pulled out the Bowie knife he kept stashed inside. After extinguishing his Zippo, he dropped to his knees and unsheathed the weapon. His life was not exciting enough that he honestly expected to be jumped by a wild animal, but he'd be a fool not to recognize that two boys had already died out here—mauled by some creature—and he was determined to be prepared. In all likelihood, he had a greater chance of running into a deputy or game warden that'd promptly harass him for squatting.

Movement. His right. His left. Dusty's meaty fist tightened around the knife handle and he kept it, blade out, at his side. His heartbeat filled his ears, his primal instinct hot and prickly. Something disturbed the leaves behind him and he spun, ignited his Zippo in his free hand and shouted, "Aha!"

The tiny flame illuminated the face of an eight-foot-tall, red-haired ape-man.

Dusty's jaw went slack. "AAAGH!"

Time froze as he struggled to understand what he was looking at. A gorilla? A bear? But a flash to childhood tales suggested something wholly different—and far more incredible.

Bigfoot.

The Bigfoot snarled and slapped the lighter out of the way, extinguishing the flame. Dusty staggered back, then raised his knife, prepared for an attack. The Bigfoot proved faster than he could comprehend and gave him a full football body check, depositing him on his backside. He lost his knife in the fall and foraged through the leafy floor in mad desperation. The Bigfoot raised its long, muscular arms and howled. Pounded once on its chest, then the ground.

Then it charged.

Dusty screamed and the beast landed on top of him, wrestling. A strong man himself, he contended with the monster, forgetting his troubles, his past, his life. He couldn't remember his own name—just the will to survive. The two of them roared and hollered, rolling on the ground, kicking up leaves and dirt. Dusty clambered onto the chest of his attacker, reared his head back and brought it down like a sledgehammer. The Bigfoot wailed, a strange echoey warble that confused Dusty's senses.

"Ack!" Dusty grabbed his head, his mind struck with pain.

The Bigfoot pushed the human off and hopped to his two, gigantic bare feet. Dusty's head cleared and he leapt for the ground, sliding along the rough terrain until the knife handle fit perfectly into his grasp. He hurried to stand, his back arched forward, a trickle of blood running down his nose.

"Come on!" he shouted, ready for more.

But the beast was gone.

He whirled to his left and saw the Bigfoot dodging behind a tree, disappearing from sight.

Movement out of the corner of his eye. He swiveled to the right just in time to see the hairy creature vanish once more.

"What is this?" he growled, his adrenaline pushing out fear. "Come on!"

A large hand slapped him on the back, painfully jerking his head back as he tripped forward. He stopped himself from falling and turned, a left hook cocked back. He swung even as he about-faced, and his hand hit the dumb face of the Bigfoot. It snorted in surprise and pain, then shook its long mane, clearing out the cobwebs.

Dusty grinned. "Yeah! Ha!"

The beast glared down at the human, moonlight reflected in its sentient and enraged eyes.

Dusty's confidence faltered. "Oh."

With one deft backhand, the Bigfoot sent him sailing through the air, smashing him against a tree trunk. Groaning, he collapsed to the ground, crawling through the foliage. Through bleary eyes, Dusty beheld the rampaging Bigfoot and simply dropped his head.

Sure, he thought. *Why not?* His life wasn't anything special—he was a burnt-out bum, slumming from town to town looking for labor. No family who'd claim him, no friends. It wasn't as if anyone would miss him if he was mauled by some Bigfoot out in the wilds of Arkansas.

Suddenly his fate sounded hilarious and Dusty laughed, coughing up blood and spit. "Yeah." He chuckled. "Why not?"

The Bigfoot placed his large hairy hands on him, hefting him to his feet, then both brute and bruiser paused. Ahead, a thin beam of light split the night sky. Strange rainbow-colored lights spilled from the crack and, impossibly, three more Bigfoot emerged. One black, one gray, and one white, all adorned in patches of what looked to be metal. Like armor. Dusty shook his bleached locks out of his face, captivated by the sight of the monster trio and the lights behind them. Through that tear in the sky, he beheld a bizarre world of red skies and brown earth and tall, spiraling sculptures that looked like clay, like termite hills. They were homes. There was *life* in there—a whole world.

Dusty gaped at the incredible sight, all but forgetting his shirt was still in the grip of the Bigfoot. "What the—?"

Then the black-furred Bigfoot spotted him.

Black-Fur threw his head back in a throaty gargle, and White- and Gray-Fur turned as one to regard him. They pointed and charged, raising staffs. *Spears.* They were made out of metal, twisted and sculpted with gruesome blades at the end. They were aiming them right at him.

"Whoa!" he shouted, struggling in the grip of the red-furred Bigfoot no doubt preparing to serve him up to its ape-men kin. "Let go of me! Let me down!"

Red-Fur kept him in a tight embrace, pulling him closer. Dusty looked up and spotted real, *human* fear in the beast's eyes as it looked back to the advancing trio. "Wait a minute . . . are they after *you?*"

Red-Fur snorted and gripped Dusty in a bear hug. There was a great whoosh of air and he felt himself being ripped from reality. A millisecond later he was standing in the forest again, but now was behind the rushing monsters, rather than in front. His head swooned and bile rose in his throat.

"What did you do?" he mumbled, swallowing vomit.

Black-Fur and his friends halted, looking about, sniffing the air. At last they settled their beady gaze on Dusty and Red-Fur, warbled once, and changed the direction of their war-charge. Gray-Fur flung his spear, and it sliced through the air with a high-pitched hum. Red-Fur pushed Dusty out of the way as the weapon stuck in a tree trunk and exploded in a spider-web of electricity. The trunk smoked, caught on fire, and split in half.

Dusty cursed, loud, scrambling in a crab-walk to inch away from the conflagration. Red-Fur was on him in an instant, lifting him to his feet and . . . *poof.*

In the blink of an eye Dusty stood at another vantage point in the forest, twenty feet away from the raging fire and the three howling Bigfoot searching the area. This time he could not help himself and he heaved his beer and jerky.

"Stop *doing* that," he croaked.

The beast quietly snorted and repeatedly poked at his shoulder.

"Cut it out," Dusty said, then realized Red-Fur was retreating deeper into the woods. "Hey," Dusty hissed. "Wait up."

He pushed past his stiff knees and sore muscles, marveling he was now trusting his former attacker with his life. Unable to turn his back to three armored Bigfoot for long, he kept looking over his shoulder. For now, Black-Fur and the two with him remained hunkered down, walking with wide gaits all around the area, sniffing, poking at bushes with their odd electro-spears, and barking commands to one another.

But they did not see Dusty, and he was grateful for that.

He smiled, then bumped into a mountain of red fur before realizing his own Bigfoot had stopped. Red-Fur snorted and jerked his matted mane toward a cliff overlooking a dense copse.

"Down there?" Dusty said, not knowing how he'd make it down the rock face.

Without waiting for an invitation, Red-Fur reached out with lumbering arms, took firm hold of his shirt and—

"No, wait!"

Poof.

Vertigo. Dusty stood, barely, at the bottom of the cliff, a heartbeat later. Red-Fur had already left him and traipsed through the thicket, aimed for a cave mouth hidden by the brush. The Bigfoot pushed aside the sticky branches, grunted at Dusty, and disappeared inside.

Dusty faced the dark maw of the cave, weighing his options.

He followed.

◆   ◆   ◆

Dusty followed the Bigfoot for another twenty minutes on foot or "teleporting" when the creature thought the puny human was lagging behind. He was beginning to get used to the disorienting leaps across distances, now understanding why, in the stories, folks only caught glimpses of a Bigfoot. But that didn't explain *where* they came from.

What are they? He thought of the panoramic red and pink sky that he glimpsed through the portal of light. *Was that an alien world? Are Bigfoots aliens? From some other dimension?*

It was a ridiculous thought, but this seemed to be his day for the ridiculous.

At last, Red-Fur led his human companion to a gutted-out husk of a shack. It looked like it'd been a cabin in a previous life, though the place was overgrown with cobwebs and weeds. The screens on the windows had been all but torn away. The place looked a good sneeze from falling over and Dusty hesitated when Red-Fur tromped onto the porch.

"Whoa, wait. What are we doing here?"

The Bigfoot did not answer, just entered the cabin. Dusty felt sure they had lost their pursuers, but he did not fancy the thought of exploring these woods alone—at night—with furry, alien killers on the loose. Taking his chances with the Bigfoot he knew, Dusty stretched his arms and went inside.

The interior of the cabin was worse than the exterior. Flies buzzed about, the smell of rotted meat funked the air, and Dusty spotted lumps of fur in one corner. A couple stray bones, an antler, and a hoof lay randomly scattered about, like crumbs dropped from a dinner table.

He spat out a curse and muffled a gag, keeping close to the open door, desperately breathing in the fresh forest air. Red-Fur didn't seem to notice the smell. Ducking to keep from scraping his head on the low ceiling, the lumbering beast crossed the house, each pad of his foot generating peals of thunder on the hard wood floor. Dusty winced through the fog of animal carcasses and spotted a messy pile of magazines and books where a kitchen table should be. Where the Bigfoot acquired such reading material, he could not imagine.

The creature searched through the mess, carelessly tossing magazines all about, selecting a small stack. He carried his selections to Dusty and gruffly shoved them into his arms.

"What?"

The beast snorted. He poked at Dusty's shoulder again—which was starting to hurt—then used a knuckle to roughly turn the pages on the top magazine.

"Okay, okay," Dusty said. He flipped through an entertainment magazine, staring blankly at stars on the red carpet and behind-the-scenes pictures from recent movie sets. "I don't know what you want me to see."

Red-Fur stopped him on a page depicting a scene from an upcoming movie. Some sort of medieval epic. The photo featured an actor decked out in regal robes and a crown, looking all majestic. Dusty was about to make a snide comment, when Red-Fur tapped the picture with a knuckle, then, with a frown, touched his own chest.

Dusty considered. "What? You're a . . . a king?"

Red-Fur nodded, his eyes haunted. He snorted out his nose, rustling Dusty's hair. Dusty was about to ask another question when the hunkered creature skulked over to an especially foul-smelling mound of fur. With massive claws, the beast reached in and brought out a handful of blood.

Dusty flinched in revulsion. "Wow."

Red-Fur dipped a finger in the blood, then began smearing it on the walls at a frantic pace.

"Whoa, calm down there, fella."

Red-Fur ignored him, drawing a circle. Then another. A couple squiggly lines later, he presented a decent kid's drawing of the planet Earth, and beside it the *other* world, Dusty assumed.

"In your world, you're a king," Dusty said again. "I get that. What are you doing *here*?"

On the drawing of the Bigfoot's world, Red-Fur made three stark lines at the top, tapped them and pointed toward the dingy windows.

"Those three guys outside? They're after you. What'd they do, chase you off?"

Red-Fur bared his teeth. Nodded. Dusty didn't like the baring teeth thing. The Bigfoot tapped the tallest of the lines—Black-Fur, if Dusty had to guess—then returned to the photo of the king in the magazine.

"The big one wants your job. Got it."

Red-Fur gestured from the other planet to Earth.

"Run you outta town, did he? Now he's here to finish the job, I'm guessing."

The Bigfoot gave a low whine. Snorted. Growled.

Dusty reasoned this was an all right dude and had a world of hurt. Who knew, maybe he wasn't the one who killed those kids. Maybe they ran afoul of Black-Fur. That guy seemed to have no trouble killing whatever came in his path.

"Look, I appreciate what you got going on here," Dusty said, handing the magazines back to Red-Fur, "but I got my own problems, brother. I got—" He was about to finish with "a life," but was that true? What was really waiting for him out there beyond the forest? The only thing he had left in this world was a son he'd abandoned out of guilt and shame. A son who, no doubt, was done waiting for him to return, no matter what Mark thought.

I'm going nowhere, he realized.

Red-Fur rumbled, as if distressed, and sat down in the middle of the cabin, head slumped, eyes distant.

Dusty supposed his new Bigfoot friend wasn't going anywhere either. Two drifters, far from home, unable to return. Exiled.

"Hey, pal—"

The window exploded in a plume of glass shards and a white giant landed squarely inside. Dusty dropped to the floor, shielding his eyes and looked up in horror as White-Fur swatted at the air with large black claws, snapping and barking. Red-Fur was up in an instant and locked with White-Fur in an arm hold. The giants wrestled, each trying to bite the other; Dusty could do nothing but watch.

The front door kicked open and Gray-Fur stomped through, holding his spear.

"Great."

The thing noticed him, roared, and stabbed at him with the spear. Dusty dodged out of the way, the edge of the blade piercing the hardwood floor. He backed against a wall, really wishing he had his knife. He waited for Red-Fur to save the day, but the beast was struggling under the might of the other Bigfoot.

Ah, screw it.

As Gray-Fur advanced, Dusty gave a battle cry of his own and tackled the beast to the ground. The monster was a gray whirlwind of fur and claws. Dusty felt small scratches on his back, his neck, and his arms.

This thing is going to tear me apart.

He brought up both fists, clasped them together, and drove them down into the thing's flat snout. Blood burst everywhere and Dusty repeated the move. Again. Wild instinct took over as he hammered at the monster, until one swipe from Gray-Fur's massive arm landed him on the floor.

Dazed, he stood, feeling weak, stinging cuts all over his body. He spotted the spear still stuck in the floor and raced for it. With all his might, he wrenched it free of the wood, just as Gray-Fur reached out for him with hooked, bloodstained claws. Dusty screamed and plunged the spear through the creature's gut until it popped out the other side, covered in gore.

Gray-Fur gurgled blood and continued to swing with his claws, but Dusty eased back and watched the beast die. "Ha! Yeah!"

He looked to Red-Fur just in time to see the Bigfoot grapple White-Fur's jaws with both hands and give a good hard yank. White-Fur's head swiveled at an impossible angle. He gasped once and collapsed in a dead heap.

"Way to go, buddy!"

Red-Fur heaved deep, ragged breaths, but managed to snort his approval at Dusty's accomplishment.

A crackling spear zoomed through the doorway, slashing Red-Fur's arm. He howled and fell sideways, and the spear dug deep into the wall. There was an explosion of light, and a burst of incredible power halved the cabin. Flames blossomed everywhere, filling the cabin with black smoke. Dusty hacked against the fumes, and reeled toward Red-Fur.

"Come on!" He helped him to his feet, straining under the Bigfoot's enormous weight.

Red-Fur followed and the two broke free of the hungry flames into the cool dark outside. The cabin went up like so much dry kindling, and Dusty collapsed to the ground, still coughing. Red-Fur moaned. Growled. Roared.

Terrified, Dusty lifted his head and beheld Black-Fur, waiting there for them, feral.

The two Bigfoot Alpha males bared their teeth and garbled a heated conversation. Dusty forced himself to stand. He'd come too far now to back out of this. The world had moved on without him, but here, left behind in its shadow, he had finally made a friend.

Friends don't run.

Red-Fur paused in his snarling tirade to regard Dusty. He snorted once, grateful, almost, then swatted him. Dusty sailed through the air, landing twenty feet away.

Before he blacked out, he saw the two Bigfoot hurling toward each other like two Mack trucks.

◆   ◆   ◆

When Dusty came to, his head felt like it'd swollen to the size of Detroit. His thoughts were muddled, his sight fuzzy. Weakly, he stood and surveyed the damage. Dawn had come. The cabin was nothing but smoking ashes.

Red-Fur sat on the ground, slumped over, his back to him.

Not moving.

"No . . ." Dusty fought through his fatigue, his pain, and hurried to his friend, but when he reached him, he hesitated. Red-Fur was weeping. In his arms lay Black-Fur, four deep gashes across his throat. He'd bled out. Died.

Red-Fur was *mourning* him.

Dusty was unsure how to proceed. "Hey . . . you okay?"

The Bigfoot snorted. Sniffed. Whined.

"I . . . I'm sorry. I don't understand you."

With speed that belied his large size, Red-Fur reached up for Dusty's shirt, grabbing it tight. Dusty feared his death was upon him, but the Bigfoot only grabbed the photo that Dusty had stashed there. Had the Bigfoot been watching him last night, in his quiet reflection?

The beast used a knuckle, jabbed at the picture of Dusty's boy. Then, gently, the creature stroked a thumb across Black-Fur's creased brow.

Dusty understood.

"Your son . . ."

Red-Fur bent low, touched his head to his cub's. Dusty's heart broke. He looked at the picture of himself and his baby. A baby he had showered with love so long ago.

I just left him. He needed me and I left.

Red-Fur stood to his full stature and gently picked up the body of his son. Then, he leveled his human-like eyes at Dusty and communicated something to him. Something profound. They had a bond, but more than that, Red-Fur seemed to see directly into Dusty's heart. All his doubts, his fears of what he'd find if he went looking for his son, his worries that it was too late to be the father he'd always meant to be.

Red-Fur struggled, his lips turning awkwardly, and simply pronounced, "Son."

Dusty wept, broken and free.

The same rainbow split appeared in thin air, just as before, and Red-Fur, with his son in his arms, crossed over into another world. Going back home. Red-Fur regarded his human friend one last time, gave a swift nod, which Dusty returned, then vanished.

Dusty did not move for a half hour.

◆　◆　◆

Dusty's worn boots kicked along the highway, his backpack weighing heavy on his shoulders. He had a whole day ahead of him and a lot of ground to cover. The rumble of an engine grew louder behind him and he turned, jerking out his thumb.

An old work truck, its back loaded down with chickens, slowed to a stop. A craggy-faced man missing most of his top teeth greeted him with barely an interest.

"Where ya headed?" the man asked.

Dusty did not hesitate. There was only one place he wanted to go.

"California." He beamed. "Gonna go see my son."

INCIDENT AT HOBB'S END

BY

BRUCE L. PRIDDY

LARRY SKAGGS, 35, and Alex Skaggs, 8, were reported missing by Skaggs' ex-wife Rosie on August 10, 2009. Initially, the Redfern County, Kentucky, Sheriff's Department suspected Skaggs had kidnapped his son, the result of a custody dispute gone wrong. However, a subsequent search of Larry Skaggs' home recovered a notebook containing startling and disturbing information. Having heard an interview on a late-night radio program about my investigations of paranormal phenomena in Kentucky, the sheriff contacted me for assistance. He sent me the notebook in hopes I could provide some insight into Mr. Skaggs' mental state and Alex's possible whereabouts. What follows are excerpts from that notebook. Please note coarse language has been removed. Commentary follows as endnotes. - Bruce L. Priddy

July 15, 2009

I knew it weren't no cougar that killed Petersen's livestock. Ain't no cougar can pull apart a bull like that. Sheriff Hart was blowing smoke up our ***** when he pronounced one was responsible without so much as waiting for the vet from the University of Kentucky to take a look. And that man had no idea what he was talking about when he tried to tell us that caterwauling we've been hearing in the woods the past two weeks was a cougar or coyotes. ****, cougars ain't been seen in Kentucky, much less Redfern County, in sixty years. [1]

I said as much to Hart, and I know everyone else agreed. He just scoffed at me. "You ever see a cougar attack, Larry?" Said it like I was stupid. He just chuckled at me when I asked him the same. If he weren't behind that badge, he'd have found my fist in his nose. Just because that incompetent sack of **** wears a star, don't mean he knows any more than the rest of us.

But last night in the woods, I saw the thing that's been getting at Petersen's livestock. It was a Bigfoot! It tears me I can't even tell anyone, "I told you so!" People'll think, between losing my job and the divorce, I've finally snapped. I've heard how those people who saw the aliens in

Hopkinsville back in the '50s were treated. [2] And Rosie . . . that *****
will use any excuse to keep Alex away from me. Still, I think I should get
my thoughts straight. Maybe if anyone else sees the monster, I can show
them what I've written. We can compare notes and we'll all know we
ain't crazy.

I was out in the woods last night 'cause Sheriff Hart asked the
community's help finding the "cougar." Hart may be stupid, but my
property borders Petersen's, so I wasn't about to take chances. I got a kid
and a dog to think about. Earlier in the day I drove down to the IGA in
Hobb's End, picked up a side of beef from the butcher. I figured if the
thing likes killing cattle, a side of beef would be good bait.

'Round sundown I set a trap in a clearing in the woods between my
land and Petersen's. I planted an old scaffolding pole in the center of the
clearing, strung the bait about eight feet up. No critter would be able to
get ahold of it but would make a big show trying, giving me plenty of
time to get a good, clear shot. I set myself up a blind in a tree at the edge
of the clearing.

I expected to see coyotes come sniffing around, but didn't see a one.
For a bit, that kinda made me think maybe Hart was right. If a cougar
was around, it'd be sure to run off the other big predators. Every other
animal was out though. The woods were busy last night. The moon was
full and bright. I'd have no trouble seeing anything come into the
clearing.

About 3:30, I heard that awful caterwaul. I couldn't tell where it was
coming from. It seemed to come from the sky, the ground, the trees and
all spaces between. The sound attacked me, punched me in the gut and
stung my nostrils. I went dizzy, almost fell from the tree. A little bit of
piss leaked out of me, I'm man enough to admit. Every part of my being
screamed at me to run, but the idea of running blind through the woods
with no idea where the caterwaul was coming from was a whole hell of a
lot more frightening. A couple of deer went crashing through the brush
below me. Across the clearing, a flock of birds rose from the trees,
crying. [3]

Then, silence. That's when I got really scared. I've ain't ever heard
the woods go that quiet.

A fog walked into the clearing. That's the only way to describe it. The
fog *walked*. It'd surge forward in fits, so fast I couldn't actually see it
move, as if I was watching it through a strobe light. As bright as the
moon was, the fog should've been bone-white, but it was the blackest
black, looked more like oil than a fog. [4]

And the smell! I ain't never smelled anything like that. It was bad eggs, decaying road-kill and an open-sewer. [5] My stomach came up into my mouth, but I was able to choke it back down. I spat out a few chunks, wiped my mouth on my sleeve, and looked back through my rifle's scope to the bait. I couldn't believe what I saw next.

The fog reached up toward the bait, forming a column. Then it sloughed away, revealing a monster inside. It looked every bit like the Bigfoot in those movies and monster-hunting shows on the cable TV. Seeing it in real-life, though, Bigfoot is almost comical. It's got this huge upper body, two or three of me across, with a big mane 'round its face and shoulders. Then it's got this tiny waist and legs; so small I kinda wondered how it held up the rest of its body. What I didn't know is that Bigfoot has a face like a dog and a big, bushy tail. But it does! [6]

I must've made some noise in fright or excitement because the Bigfoot looked right down my scope at me. It has these terrible, red-as-Hell eyes. Those "experts" on those monster-hunting shows say Bigfoot is just an animal. That's a bunch of bull-****. I knew right then, seeing those eyes, Bigfoot ain't no animal.

We made eye contact and it spoke in my head! *"Put down your weapon. Come to me."* I heard it as I do my own thoughts. Thing is, it sounded like a good idea. I almost did.

I remember when I was five, a walking pneumonia hit me hard. My daddy read to me from a children's book about Bigfoot while we sat in the pediatrician's office waiting to see the doctor. There was this part where a hunter says he got Bigfoot in his sights but couldn't pull the trigger 'cause the monster looked "too human." When I heard that voice in my head, knew what it was trying do to me, I had no such qualms. I nailed that son-of-a-**** right between his hellfire-and-brimstone eyes.

I know the bullet hit because the monster's head jerked backwards, then it fell. And I heard it hit, too. First time I ever heard a bullet hit a living target. It was a clang, like I'd shot an empty oil drum. The sound echoed through the woods. [7]

The Bigfoot sprang back up onto all fours. It looked at me through my scope again, letting loose its awful caterwaul. I could see its fangs. They are as big as my thumbs! All that fur 'round its face and neck was standing on end. I knew if the Bigfoot got ahold of me I'd be done for. I let another shot go, aimed it right down its roaring maw.

I thought I had it that time, but I'll be damned if it didn't get right back up! This time, though, it ran back into the forest. The fog left with it, as if it was part of the monster's body. I jumped down from my blind and chased it. Not the brightest thing to do, but I guess I let the thought of the Noble Prize they'd give me for catching Bigfoot overwhelm my better judgment.

I could hear the Bigfoot crashing through the trees just ahead, maybe no more than a dozen yards or so. Thinking back now, the thing had a huge lead on me. There is no way I could've caught up. I think it might have been taunting me. It led me to a small hill. Now, I've been hunting deer in those woods for years; I don't remember any hill being there. But then again, everything is unfamiliar in the dark. Anyway, we get to this hill and, I swear on my mamma's grave, a hole opens up with bright orange light spilling out. The Bigfoot looked over its shoulder, bared its fangs and stepped into the hole. Before I could squeeze off another shot, the hole closed up. [8]

After the high from the chase wore off, the situation hit me—I'd have to walk back through the woods, in the dark, with no idea where this monster went. Like hell I was going to do that. Instead, I found my way back to the tree-blind at the clearing. Much safer there, I figured. No monster could sneak up behind me.

Sunrise came and I made my way back home. I got back a few minutes ago, had a drink to stop my shaking long enough to write this. Going to need a lot more before I can get to sleep.

July 16, 2009

I slept until about 3:30 this morning. Thought I heard a noise, but I'm probably just having nightmares. Any man who said he wouldn't after seeing what I have is a ***-**** liar. My head hurt bad. Doubt there is any Jack left in the house.

At sunrise I went back to the clearing to see if I could find a blood trail, maybe figure out where the Bigfoot went. There wasn't a drop anywhere. I plugged the monster twice, dead on. It should have been leaking something bad.

Maybe I am going crazy.

July 17, 2009

I knew I had heard something last night! Woke up again at 3:30. Raccoons got into a fight on the roof, all sorts of howling and growling. Thought they were going to come through the roof right into my lap or shake the house apart. Roscoe was going crazy. He followed the fight around the house, snarling at the ceiling the whole time. I'd never seen him so worked up.

I got my rifle and went outside. I didn't see anything up on the roof, but could still hear them carrying on. I fired a shot into the air. That scared them off. Didn't see how many there were, but heard the racket they made when they went running off into the woods. Must have been big.

Got back in the house, and found the antique lamp I inherited from my grandmama broken against a wall. Roscoe must've knocked it over trying to chase the raccoons. Can't be mad at him for trying to protect the house. Someone's going to have chicken hearts in his dinner bowl tomorrow.

July 20, 2009

Man, I am having nightmares now. Thought I had woke up and saw Bigfoot staring in my bedroom window. I wanted to get my rifle, but I couldn't move. Like those eyes had paralyzed me. I couldn't even scream. Swear that fog was in the house. Then, I felt a loud bang and could move again. Nothing was in the window. [9]

July 22, 2009

Raccoons were at it again last night. Except for hearing Roscoe's barking in my dreams, I slept right through. They must've been having a real time of it, though. Shook the house so bad they knocked pictures off the walls.

July 24, 2009

Rosie let me see Alex tonight.

We picked up some ice-cream in Hobb's End then I took him back to the house so he could play with Roscoe. When we pulled up in the driveway, we could see Roscoe in the front room window, barking all sorts of crazy.

Alex said, "Look, Dad! Look!" pointing into the woods.

Big globes of glowing orange light were dancing through the trees. It was beautiful and terrifying at the same time. We watched them for about fifteen minutes before they flew over the treetops and disappeared in a bright flash. From the looks of it, right before they vanished, the lights were over the clearing where I saw the Bigfoot.

Alex asked me what the lights were. I told him they were swamp gas.

Like hell they were. [10]

July 27, 2009

Had a job interview this morning, or at least I was supposed to. When I got there, the plant manager said the interview was canceled. He said they received a phone call that I was being investigated and was told it would be in the company's best interest not to hire me.

Rosie thinks she's cute, but keeping me from getting a job ain't going to help her out any. How does that stupid ***** think I'm going to pay her child support if I'm not making any money? I'd love to lay into her dumb ***, but she won't let me see Alex this weekend if I say even one cross word to her.

July 28, 2009

The caterwaul woke me up at 3:30. Outside, I saw those red-as-all-hell eyes in the woods, watching the house. That damned fog skirted the edge of my yard. I went out on the porch, fired a few rounds into the woods. I know the bullets hit. The clangs were loud. Like someone flicking a switch, the eyes disappeared. Thought that meant I'd scared the S.O.B. away.

I went back inside, wanting a drink to fix my nerves. No sooner than I had the door shut the attack started. Heavy fists pounded against the siding, shaking the whole house. The door knobs twisted like they were trying to come in. Stomping and scratching on the roof followed me from room to room. Roscoe flew between fits of maddened rage and cowering between my feet.

I took my rifle and Roscoe into the bathroom, the only room in the house with no windows, to wait for what I thought was the end of my life. But it didn't come. Outside the bathroom, I heard my house being ransacked. The knob on the bathroom door turned, but it never opened. Above me I thought the Bigfoot was going to come through the roof. How could one monster do all that alone? I know I've only seen one and there was only one pair of eyes in the woods last night, but there has to be more.

If the Bigfoot wanted to get me, I'd be dead. A creature that big—nothing could stop it getting at me. Except, it didn't. I think the monster is just screwing with me, as if I was entertainment.

The attack lasted an hour. I didn't dare come out of the bathroom until well after sunrise. Everything I own has been destroyed. The kitchen table was split in half, the chairs only good for firewood now. Every dish and bottle of whiskey is out of the cabinet and broken on the floor. The HD TV I got for Christmas is broken, the entertainment center on top of it. All my clothes are shredded. The mattresses on my bed and Alex's bed have been ripped open, the springs pulled out. All the pictures Rosie allowed me to keep are out of their frames and look like they have bite marks in them. Big holes have been punched in the walls. Some of them look like they were chewed through. My phone is broken, the cord ripped right out of the wall. I'd take a picture of the damage of it all, but the son of a ***** broke my camera too.

I don't know how it happened. I heard the Bigfoot in the house. The evidence, everything I've worked for my whole life is on the floor around me, ruined. But, the front and back doors are still locked, just as I left them! Every window is still in one piece! How the hell is this possible? Can it teleport through walls? [11]

Even if Hart is an ***-****, I don't have too much pride to not admit when I need help. I'm going down to Hobb's End to file a report. I'm in over my head here. Don't give two ***** if people think I'm crazy.

◆ ◆ ◆

Am I being bugged? If I am, I wouldn't even know where to start looking. Where in the hell would it be hidden? Everything I own's been destroyed.

It can't be a bug. That wouldn't make any sense. I didn't actually *say* I was going to see Hart, I only wrote it. How did they know?

I never made it to the Sheriff's Office. I got about half-way to Hobb's End when I got pulled over by an old black Cadillac. The design of the car had to be about sixty years old, but it was in top shape, like it'd just rolled out of the factory. The shine was so bright the car was hard to look at. It didn't look like no police car, but it had one of those old single bubble lights on top, so of course I pulled over for it.

The guys who got out of the car certainly weren't no cops. There were three of them, as tall as they were skinny. Walking scarecrows. They were wearing really nice, black suits about three sizes too big. Those suits probably fit the hangers better. Ain't a one looked like he'd even heard of the sun before. But the one thing I noticed the most were their Jimmy Durant noses protruding out from under wrap-around shades. [12]

One man walked around to my door, while the two others hung around the trunk of my car. I could feel their eyes crawling along my back. The one at my door motioned for me to roll down the window. When I did, he leaned in and shoved his face into mine. He grinned, as if he was enjoying some sort of private joke. Up close, his skin looked like wax. And, oh, he carried the stink of the fog on him! I was nauseous the entire time he spoke.

The words didn't match his lips. His voice sounded far away and full of static, like an old radio offset from a signal.

There was no mistaking what he was saying, though. He told me if I ever said a word to anyone about what was happening, Alex would be taken away, and it'd be best if I turned my car around and went home. [13]

Next thing I know, I've parked my car on my front lawn. I don't remember the men getting back into their car or the drive home. Only thing I remember is the sound of his voice, how every word sounded like the best idea I'd ever heard.

What the hell is happening to me?

Am I going crazy or do they just want me to think I am?

July 31, 2009

I'm supposed to have Alex for the weekend. It ain't safe here, though. We're going to drive up to my brother's in Louisville for a couple of days. Alex'll enjoy playing with his cousins. I could use a beer and a good night's sleep. Haven't slept since Monday.

August 3, 2009

Nowhere is safe.

When we got to my brother's, Michael was surprised to see us there. He said I had called an hour before to say we weren't going to make it. Michael said the number on his caller ID was my home number, which is impossible since it takes almost two hours to get to Louisville. Thinking I was putting him on, Michael laughed it off.

We had the cops out at Michael's twice. Both nights after we all went to bed, we heard someone on the roof and scratching at the windows.

Scared the absolute hell out of the kids. Michael's little girl saw someone trying to peek in her bedroom window. By the time we got outside, this "person" was gone. She said she saw the person on all fours. Michael wrote it off as the person crouching. I didn't correct him, never mind her telling us the man's head reached the top of her window. The cops showed and the noises stopped. But as soon as they left, the noises started again, lasting until dawn.

Rosie laid into me when I dropped Alex off at her place. She said I had been calling her and hanging up every fifteen minutes, all weekend. We fought, said a lot of nasty things to each other. Alex hid in his room. Even over our screaming, I could hear him crying. Rosie said I wouldn't ever see him again. [12]

May be for the best.

August 5, 2009

Roscoe is dead.

He woke me up around 3 A.M., all sorts of barks and snarling. Out the window I saw a pair of glowing red eyes in the trees. I was tired, I hadn't slept and I was pissed-off. I decided right then this was going to be the night I found out how many bullets it took to kill a Bigfoot. When I stepped outside, Roscoe ran out between my legs, almost knocking me over. He disappeared into the night. I heard him fighting something. Then, a squeal. I ain't ever heard an animal make a noise like that before. It was absolute pain.

I ran back inside the house. I couldn't listen to my best friend being tortured. Sitting on the couch, I watched the trees out the living room window, hoping Roscoe'd come running back. Instead, the monster came. It walked like an ape, using the knuckles on one hand to support itself. The monster carried something in the other, clutched to its chest. I swear, the son-of-***** smiled at me.

It sat just at the edge of the light coming from the house. It tossed Roscoe on the ground. He was still alive, but hurt bad. Judging from the way he dragged himself along the ground, his back hips were broken. He tried crawling to the house. The Bigfoot yanked him back. Roscoe howled in agony. One by one, the Bigfoot ripped off Roscoe's legs. I ran to the door, fired a shot at the Bigfoot. The bullet knocked the Bigfoot on its back. The monster leapt to all fours and roared at me. I fired another round. There was a loud *clang!* but the monster didn't move. It picked up Roscoe's body and threw it at me, hitting me in the face with the bleeding remains of my dog. My nose broke. I puked.

The monster disappeared. I fired every round I had into the woods, begging God that I hit something, to let me kill the thing that hurt my dog. Roscoe was still breathing, twitching. I had to smother my best friend to put him out of his misery. There was nothing left in my stomach, but that didn't stop my body from trying to puke again.

Why didn't the monster kill me? It had me dead to rights while I was getting sick. Doesn't matter if I was getting sick or not, it could have easily ripped me apart. Why didn't it?

That's what Sheriff Hart asked me when I called him out (I picked up a pre-paid cellphone up in Louisville). I don't care what those men from the Caddy said, I need help. Hart saw Roscoe's body, saw what the Bigfoot did to him, but I don't think he believed a word I was saying. Kept asking me if I was sure it wasn't a cougar. Finally he said, "I believe you believe you saw something."

Condescending bastard. He said he'd have to wait until morning to go hunt the monster in the woods.

Coward.

August 9, 2009

I've lost Alex.

Rosie showed up on my door about 9 o'clock, saying she'd been called into work. I got pissed because she hadn't called first. She said she tried, but it went straight to voice mail. I asked if her mother could keep Alex. Of course, she said she couldn't get ahold of her mother either. [15]

As soon as she was gone, I packed up Alex and got in the car. Alex asked where we were going. I have no idea where I intended to take us, but we couldn't stay here, so I told him we were getting some ice cream. The car wouldn't start. Nothing happened when I turned the key. I tried to stay calm, so Alex wouldn't be scared. He saw through it, kept asking me what was wrong. I told him I was sick. Don't know if he bought it.

Back inside, I tried calling everyone I know for help. My phone wasn't getting any service. Without a TV to keep him occupied, Alex followed me around the house, whining that he was bored. I told him to read all those books he begged me to buy for him and had so far refused to open.

Fortunately, he didn't stay awake long. Ten rolled around and he was ready for bed. With our sleeping bags and a battery-operated lantern, I made us a little camp in his bedroom. Alex fell asleep reading a *Goosebumps* book by lantern-light. Soon as I was certain he was asleep, I snuck my rifle into the room to keep watch. A radio was there to keep me company, keep me awake. It didn't work. I dozed off leaning against my rifle.

A noise at the front door slapped me awake. Alex's sleeping bag was empty. I ran into the front door to find Alex trying to open the door.

I scooped him up away from the door, screaming at him. "What the hell are you doing, boy?"

Even in the dark, I could see a glaze over his eyes. He swayed on his feet, threatened to topple over. "The monster at the window told me to come outside." His voice was far away.

I peeked out through the blinds on the front window. That black fog was invading the yard. On the tree line, a set of hellfire eyes watched the house.

I carried Alex to the bathroom, locked him inside.

He screamed. "I need to go outside! I need to go outside!"

I put my back to the bathroom door, rifle trained down the hallway leading to the front room. No monster was going to get my boy.

I failed. They got him and he's probably dead now 'cause I'm a screw-up.

The house shook, something heavy beat against all four sides. Shingles were being torn off the roof. The horrible caterwaul echoed through the house, sounded like it came from inside. Alex howled in response. His voice was all animal rage. I about pissed myself. Alex beat on the bathroom door, with a force unnatural for a child his size. The wood began to split.

I opened the door. Huge gashes ran across his forehead, pouring blood down his face. Clumps of blood and hair stuck to the door. Trying to fight tears and panic, I cradled him to me. "Oh buddy, what did you do to yourself?" Those were my last words to him.

He transformed. Not my son any longer, but a fury of teeth and fingernails. He bit deep into my shoulder, raked at my face and eyes, left ragged furrows on my cheeks. I threw him away from me. A chunk of my shoulder came away in his mouth. It hasn't stopped gushing.

Alex bared his teeth at me and hissed. He ran to the front door and ripped it open, the wood around the lock splintering. The last time I saw my son he was running into forest on all fours. The fog seemed to chase after him. And the eyes at the tree line watched, unmoving. I considered, for the briefest of moments, shooting Alex to spare him from the monster.

I should have. If I was man enough, if I loved him enough, I would have. I should have gone out to find him a long time ago. But I had to get this down, 'cause I know we ain't coming back, and someone has to know what happened to us. I'm going to go find my little boy . . .

If you have any information on the whereabouts of Larry Skaggs or Alex Skaggs please contact the National Center for Missing or Exploited Children or the Redfern County Sheriff's Department. Thank you. — BLP

Endnotes

1.   While the mountain lion is officially extinct in Kentucky, there were sightings of alien big cats—ABCs—coinciding with the wave of animal mutilations that swept the state through '09 and '10. Any connection remains to be seen, though I cannot help, but to suspect the deceptive nature of the paranormal at work, such as what John Keel experienced during his time in Point Pleasant, WV, a phenomenon that researcher Christopher O'Brien refers to as the Trickster.

2.   I believe Skaggs is referring to an encounter commonly known as the Hopkinsville Goblins case. In 1955, the Sutton and Taylor families reported a night-long battle with at least two grotesque, diminutive entities that repeatedly tried entering the Sutton home. Though neighbors did not see the entities, they did report seeing strange lights in the area and hearing a gunfight on the Sutton property. Hopkinsville police investigated, finding hundreds of spent shells and an unidentified glowing liquid that evaporated before samples could be taken. Project Bluebook considered the Hopkinsville Goblins case unsolved.

3.   Many paranormal events are preceded by a loud howl, in particular with Bigfoot encounters.

4.   Though a Hollywood cliché, a thick fog is a common element in paranormal events.

5.   While most often associated with demons, researchers such as John Keel and Phil Imborgno have found a sulfur-like odor to be another common element in paranormal events, reported in everything from Bigfoot and black dog sightings, to close encounters with aliens.

6.   Many researchers are starting to consider the possibility Bigfoot is a sort of paranormal meme. While anomalous apes have been a ubiquitous part of American folklore dating back to before Columbus,

there was little in the way of uniformity among descriptions of the creatures. Each region had its own version. Throughout Appalachia and the American Southeast, stories were told of a vicious anomalous ape known as the Wampus Cat to Native tribes and the Devil Monkey to white settlers. The Devil Monkey is very similar in description to a giant howler monkey or baboon. After the infamous Patterson-Gimlin film became public in October 1967, there was a steep and immediate drop in the number of reported Devil Monkey sightings. Until Larry Skaggs' July 2009 sighting, the last known sighting of a Devil Monkey was in 1975, when cryptozoologist Loren Coleman investigated reports that a group of three such creatures slaughtered a calf in Albany, Kentucky. That is not to say there have not been sightings of anomalous apes in Appalachia since then; on the contrary, a study shows the change has not been in the number of sightings, but in the description of the creature sighted. It is as if the Patterson-Gimlin film displaced and rewrote the idea of what an anomalous ape should be in the public consciousness. Why Skaggs saw a Devil Monkey in 2009 after an absence of 34 years is unknown. Since the incident at Hobb's End, the number of Devil Monkey sightings has steady increased. Given the violent nature of the beast, this trend is quite disturbing.

7.   Lucky Sutton and Billy Ray Taylor reported the same hollow clang when they shot the entities trying to invade the Sutton home. In his *Hunt for the Skinwalker*, Colm Kelleher also reports the noise was heard when Tom Gorman fired at the giant wolves that frequently attacked the livestock on his Utah ranch.

8.   A National Institute of Discovery team investigating the Skinwalker Ranch in Utah also saw anomalous apes moving in and out of similar portals.

9.   On the surface, this seems like a normal case of sleep paralysis, a sleep disorder wherein the sufferer wakes during the middle of a dream, but the body does not recognize it is awake, resulting in a momentary paralysis and hallucinations. Except for some key elements. Sleep paralysis hallucinations are usually not as vivid as Skaggs describes. And the feeling of the creature's eyes causing the paralysis is a common theme in alien abduction reports.

10.   A search of the National UFO Reporting Center's online catalogue of sightings shows five other witnesses saw these strange balls of light over Redfern County July 24th. Many cryptozoologists, especially those who insist Bigfoot is a flesh-and-blood creature, will either ignore or refuse to discuss cases of high-strangeness involving Bigfoot, perhaps

out of concern it will hurt their credibility. But such cases do exist. In 1972, Stan Gordon investigated a series of UFO sightings in Westmoreland County, PA, where Bigfoot was seen in association with the craft. Abductees under hypnosis have described Bigfoot-like creatures examining them alongside the more well-known "gray" aliens. Psychic Franek Kluski witnessed a "strange creature between ape and man," and smelling of a wet-dog, that materialized in his study during a series of séances held in 1919. Kluski is not the only psychic to have seen such a manifestation.

11.   Though not often mentioned in the literature, both Bigfoot and UFO witnesses will report poltergeist activity in their homes soon after their sighting. Why this happens is unclear. I cannot help but to think that Mr. Skaggs experienced an extreme manifestation of this, not only on this night, but on several nights previous.

12.   Known by a more popular name due to a series of blockbuster summer movies, John Keel refers to such men as "doll-people." Keel (and researchers that followed) observed these men appeared to be more artificial construct than living/breathing beings. Popular culture associates them with UFO sightings, but doll-people have been known to engage in a campaign of harassment against witnesses of many types of paranormal phenomena.

13.   Loren Coleman has investigated dozens of what he calls "phantom social workers." This appears to be a common tactic used against witnesses of paranormal phenomenon, used not only by doll-people but seemingly normal human beings as well. A witness will be approached by a stranger who either threatens to take their children away if they tell anyone about what they saw, or demanding the witness hand over their children, saying it is in the child's best interest. To date, and perhaps fortunately, no one has yet to do so. Police looking into "phantom social worker" cases have produced no leads and in every case local child-welfare officials deny they are investigating the witness.

14.   During his Mothman investigation, John Keel also suffered a phantom that would call Keel's friends and family, mimicking his voice.

15.   Rosie Skaggs works as a nurse at Redfern County's Vallee Hospital. Sheriff Hart found that the hospital had not called Ms. Skaggs in, but let her pick up an extra shift when she arrived. Phone records indicate no calls were made from her phone to either Larry Skaggs or her mother.

About the Editors

Eric S. Brown is the author of numerous books including the *Bigfoot War* series, *The War of the Worlds Plus Blood Guts and Zombies*, *Season of Rot*, and *World War of the Dead* to name only a few. His short fiction has been published hundreds of times in the small press and beyond. He lives in NC with his wife and kids, where he continues to write as many tales of the hungry dead, blazing guns, and the things that lurk in the woods. Visit his Website at **ericsbrown.wordpress.com**

A.P. Fuchs is the author of many novels and short stories, most of which have been published. His most recent books are the action-packed superhero novel, *Axiom-man: City of Ruin*, the supernatural zombie novel, *Redemption of the Dead* (the final book in *The Undead World Trilogy*), and *Zombie Fight Night: Battles of the Dead*, in which zombies fight such classic monsters as werewolves, vampires, Bigfoot, and even go up against awesome foes like pirates, ninjas, and . . . Bruce Lee. Fuchs lives and writes in Winnipeg, Manitoba. Visit him on the Web at **www.canisterx.com**

About the Authors

Larry Berreth lives in Colorado with his wife, two sons, and two very tricky basset hounds. He writes online columns for Examiner.com as the Longmont Zombie Examiner and the Denver Dog News Examiner. Larry enjoys craft beer, hiking, and has an abundant comic book collection. He has occasionally gone overboard on his Halloween and Christmas decorations, and is currently at work on his first novel.

Rebecca Besser is the author of *Undead Drive-Thru, Nurse Blood,* and *Hall of Twelve*. She writes fiction, nonfiction, and poetry for various age groups and genres. Her work has appeared in a variety of mediums including magazines, ezines, blogs, websites, books, and anthologies. To learn more about her visit her website: **www.rebeccabesser.com**

A.M. Burns lives in the Colorado Rockies with his partner, several dogs, cats, horses, and birds. When he's not writing, he's often fixing fences, hiking in the mountains, or flying his hawks. You can find out more about A.M. and his writing at **www.amburns.com**, or follow him on Twitter @am_burns

Jason Rodimus Fowler was born in the summer of 1976 and hails from Raleigh, North Carolina. He has had a passion for horror and the absurd since he was a small child, which he blames in part on his babysitters, who just happened to have been Monty Python and Rod Serling via the television. His twisted tales of fear and retribution range from battling hordes of the undead, to true love among demon fodder.

Paul A. Freeman is the author of *Rumours of Ophir*, a novel set in Zimbabwe which is presently on that country's high school English Literature syllabus. He writes largely crime and horror fiction, and his short stories have been widely published. His narrative poem-novella, *Robin Hood and Friar Tuck: Zombie Killers - A Canterbury Tale* was published in 2009 by Coscom Entertainment, and his crime novel, *Vice and Virtue*, set in Saudi Arabia, was published in 2010 in German translation by Pulp Master. Currently, he works in Abu Dhabi, where he lives with his wife and three children. He can be found online at **www.paulfreeman.weebly.com**

Keith Gouveia is a mechanical engineer who writes fiction in his spare time. His latest releases, *Animal Behavior and Other Tales of Lycanthropy* and *The Black Cat and the Ghoul* have been well received and come highly recommended. Also, if you are a fan of the short story format, he recommends The Snuff Syndicate, a multi-authored novel in which serial killers have created their own social network, now available from Beating Windward Press.

Bryan Hall is a horror and dark fiction writer living in the mountains of North Carolina in a one-hundred-year-old farmhouse he desperately wishes was haunted. His fiction has appeared in numerous magazines and anthologies as well as the collection, *Whispers From the Dark*, and his debut novel, *Containment Room 7*, is now available from Permuted Press. You can visit him online at **www.bryanhallfiction.com**

Jack Hessey hails from Mansfield in England and is currently a student at Nottingham Trent University. He has three novels published, a Children's Fantasy story called *On Angels Wings*, a steampunk novel called

Steam Queen and a superhero fantasy story called *True Hero*? His biggest inspirations are Philip Reeve, J.K Rowling and Jack London.

Bowie V. Ibarra is an author living in Texas. He earned a BFA in Acting and an MA in Theatre History. His works include the zombie horror series, *Down the Road*, the action/adventure story, *Codename: La Lechusa*, and the horror tribute, *Big Cat*. You can network with Bowie and explore his works at **ZombieBloodFights.com**

S. Nycole Laff fell in love with the horror genre at the age of ten, and has been a fan ever since. Recently she has started writing and publishing her own dark and twisted tales, with this story marking her first appearance in an anthology. She lives in the desert with her remarkably tolerant husband, three cats, and two dogs.

Kevin Millikin lives in Marysville, Washington with his fiancé and a small menagerie of cats where they are also expecting their first child. Over the last couple years, his short stories have appeared in numerous anthologies. His upcoming work include the zombie novel, *Summer of '68* you can find him online at **facebook.com/kevin.millikin**

Greg Mitchell is the author of *The Strange Man*—the first book in *The Coming Evil Trilogy*—released in 2011 by Realms Fiction. He has seen his short stories published in editions of *The Midnight Diner*, as well as on StarWars.com and HalloweenComics.com. He lives in Paragould, Arkansas, with his wife and two daughters, where he has yet to see a Bigfoot . . . but he hopes to someday, provided they're as cool as Red-Fur. Greg can be found lurking on his blog at **www.thecomingevil.blogspot.com**

Bruce L. Priddy is a writer, editor and father living in Louisville, KY. His writing can be found at *Morpheus Tales*, *MicroHorror* and the *Lovecraft eZine* among other places. He also edits the flash-fiction website EschatologyJournal.org. He also loves karaoke. Buy him a drink if you see him out and about.

J.W. Schnarr is a horror writer originally from Calgary, Alberta, Canada. He is the author of the novel *Alice & Dorothy* as well as the short fiction collection, *Things Falling Apart*. A member of the HWA and SF Canada, he can be seen lurking in places such as *Best New Zombie Tales* Volume II

(Books of the Dead Press) where *Rue Morgue* magazine dubbed his story "Freshest Tale" of the anthology. He's also been spotted in *Andromeda Spaceways Inflight Magazine* and will soon be found in *Slices of Flesh* (Dark Moon Books) alongside the likes of Ramsey Campbell and Jack Ketchum. Schnarr has a space at *Black Glove Magazine* where he writes a monthly editorial titled "The Hand That Reads." By day he works as a reporter and photographer for the *Claresholm Local Press* in Claresholm, Alberta. Look him up on Facebook, Twitter, or Goodreads, or check out his blog at **jwschnarr.blogspot.com**

D.G. Sutter is a writer and editor living in Massachusetts. His work has appeared in the anthologies, *Seasons in the Abyss, Putrid Poetry & Sickening Sketches,* and *Alienology: Tales from the Void* (which he also edited). When not writing he can be found in the woods of New England, seeking irrefutable proof of the hairy legend. Keep up with him at **www.dgsutter.wordpress.com**

Sheri White is a writer from Jefferson, MD. When not writing, she is reading, reviewing, or editing. She has three girls, and has been successful in her attempts to bring them into the horror fold. When she is online, which is almost all the time, she can be found on Facebook. Feel free to email her at **sheriw1965@yahoo.com**

Thrillers, Suspense, Horror . . .

. . . this is what we do.

Browse our Catalog at Coscom Entertainment Online
Bringing You the Very Best in Quality Fiction
www.coscomentertainment.com

All books available in paperback and eBook at your favorite
online retailer like Amazon.com